The Cat and the King

Also by
Louis Auchincloss

FICTION

The Indifferent Children
The Injustice Collectors
Sybil
A Law for the Lion
The Romantic Egoists
The Great World and Timothy Colt
Venus in Sparta
Pursuit of the Prodigal
The House of Five Talents
Portrait in Brownstone
Powers of Attorney
The Rector of Justin
The Embezzler
Tales of Manhattan
A World of Profit
Second Chance
I Come as a Thief
The Partners
The Winthrop Covenant
The Dark Lady
The Country Cousin
The House of the Prophet

NONFICTION

Reflections of a Jacobite
Pioneers and Caretakers
Motiveless Malignity
Edith Wharton
Richelieu
A Writer's Capital
Reading Henry James
Life, Law and Letters
Persons of Consequence: Queen Victoria
and Her Circle

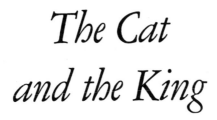

The Cat
and the King

LOUIS AUCHINCLOSS

Weidenfeld and Nicolson · London

For Jacqueline Kennedy Onassis,
who persuaded me that Versailles
was still a valid source for fiction.

Copyright © 1981 by Louis Auchincloss

First published in Great Britain in 1981 by
George Weidenfeld and Nicolson Ltd
91 Clapham High Street
London sw4

Printed in Great Britain by
Redwood Burn Limited, Trowbridge & Esher

ISBN 0 297 77989 3

"A cat may look at a king."
— Old proverb

The House of Bourbon

Louis XIII
(d. 1643)

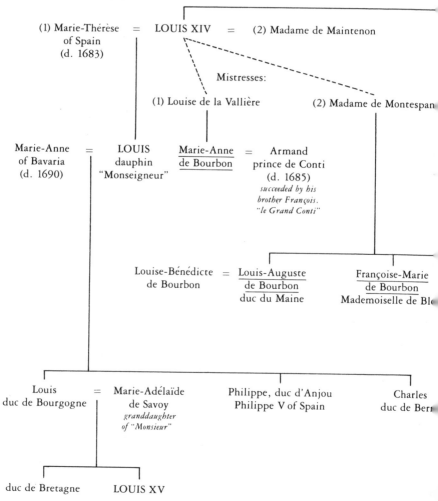

(1) Marie-Thérèse = LOUIS XIV = (2) Madame de Maintenon
of Spain
(d. 1683)

Mistresses:

(1) Louise de la Vallière   (2) Madame de Montespan

Marie-Anne = LOUIS   Marie-Anne = Armand
of Bavaria   dauphin   de Bourbon   prince de Conti
(d. 1690)   "Monseigneur"   (d. 1685)
succeeded by his
brother François,
"le Grand Conti"

Louise-Bénédicte = Louis-Auguste   Françoise-Marie
de Bourbon   de Bourbon   de Bourbon
duc du Maine   Mademoiselle de Bl

Louis = Marie-Adélaïde   Philippe, duc d'Anjou   Charles
duc de Bourgogne   de Savoy   Philippe V of Spain   duc de Berr
granddaughter
of "Monsieur"

duc de Bretagne   LOUIS XV

at the time of Saint-Simon's Narration

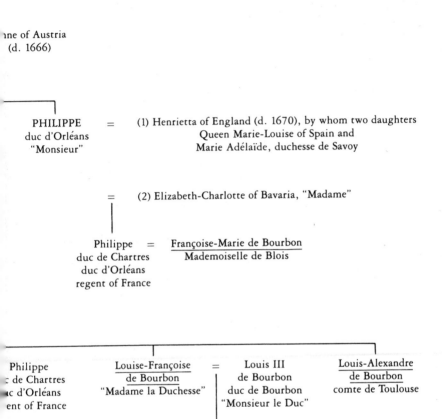

ıne of Austria
(d. 1666)

PHILIPPE   =   (1) Henrietta of England (d. 1670), by whom two daughters
duc d'Orléans   Queen Marie-Louise of Spain and
"Monsieur"   Marie Adélaïde, duchesse de Savoy

=   (2) Elizabeth-Charlotte of Bavaria, "Madame"

Philippe   =   Françoise-Marie de Bourbon
duc de Chartres   Mademoiselle de Blois
duc d'Orléans
regent of France

Philippe   Louise-Françoise   =   Louis III   Louis-Alexandre
⸝ de Chartres   de Bourbon   de Bourbon   de Bourbon
ıc d'Orléans   "Madame la Duchesse"   duc de Bourbon   comte de Toulouse
ent of France   "Monsieur le Duc"

Elizabeth   Mademoiselle de Bourbon
ıdemoiselle de Valois

Illegitimates underscored

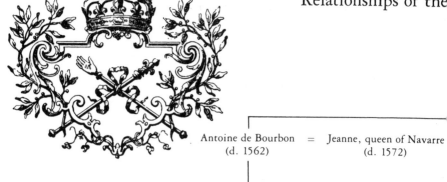

Antoine de Bourbon   =   Jeanne, queen of Navarre
(d. 1562)   (d. 1572)

Henri IV
(d. 1610)
*brought the House of Bourbon to the French throne
on extinction of Capet and Valois lines*

LOUIS XIII
(d. 1643)

LOUIS XIV

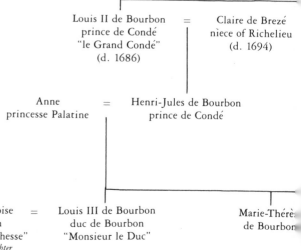

Louis II de Bourbon   =   Claire de Brezé
prince de Condé   nièce of Richelieu
"le Grand Condé"   (d. 1694)
(d. 1686)

Anne   =   Henri-Jules de Bourbon
princesse Palatine   prince de Condé

Louise-Françoise   =   Louis III de Bourbon   Marie-Thérè
de Bourbon   duc de Bourbon   de Bourbon
"Madame la Duchesse"   "Monsieur le Duc"
*legitimated daughter
of Louis XIV*

Condés and Contis to Louis XIV

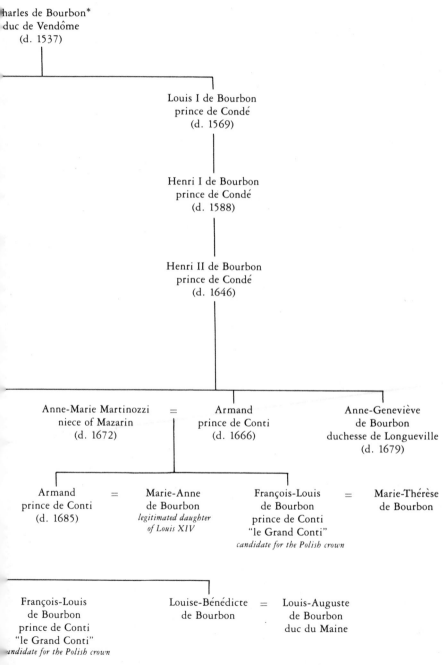

Charles de Bourbon*
duc de Vendôme
(d. 1537)

Louis I de Bourbon
prince de Condé
(d. 1569)

Henri I de Bourbon
prince de Condé
(d. 1588)

Henri II de Bourbon
prince de Condé
(d. 1646)

Anne-Marie Martinozzi   =   Armand
niece of Mazarin   prince de Conti
(d. 1672)   (d. 1666)

Anne-Geneviève
de Bourbon
duchesse de Longueville
(d. 1679)

Armand   =   Marie-Anne
prince de Conti   de Bourbon
(d. 1685)   *legitimated daughter
                     of Louis XIV*

François-Louis   =   Marie-Thérèse
de Bourbon   de Bourbon
prince de Conti
"le Grand Conti"
candidate for the Polish crown

François-Louis
de Bourbon
prince de Conti
"le Grand Conti"
candidate for the Polish crown

Louise-Bénédicte   =   Louis-Auguste
de Bourbon   de Bourbon
                       duc du Maine

*Descended in male line from Louis IX (d. 1270)

Part I

1

A YEAR AGO TODAY, the fifteenth of October, 1749, was the most important day of my now stretched-out life, even more so than the day of my wedding, or that of my sainted father's death, when I became the second duc de Saint-Simon. For it was the day on which I completed my memoirs and put away the thousands of pages of my manuscript, wrapped in eleven calfskin portfolios, each stamped with my arms, in a leather chest, to await the time, probably long after my own demise, when my heirs or representatives should deem the political and social climate appropriate for their publication. Of course, I realize that that era may never come, or if it does, that no printer may be found who is prepared to undertake so massive and costly a project. And I must also face the possibility that these portfolios, securely as I intend to have them kept, may succumb to the hazards of fire or of vandals, or may simply be destroyed or thrown away by an irresponsible descendant or a malicious or careless servant. These hazards are great, and yet I have a curiously intense, small faith burning somewhere deep within me — and which must have burned, at least to some degree, during all the years when I toiled to correlate and edit the millions of notes jotted down almost daily since the time I first came to Versailles — that these memoirs will survive to illuminate the reign of Louis XIV to generations unborn.

Has any writer, I wonder, since the beginning of time, labored so long and so arduously for a purely posthumous reward? I doubt it. But these memoirs have already fulfilled a function for me, even if they are never published. They have provided me, to put it at its simplest, with a life. They have given me a self-respect that no accomplishment or position at court could ever have given me. They have enabled me to cope with the elusive world around me by grasping it, so to speak, by the tail and smacking it down on my desk, like a flapping, slithering fish. I have been able to stand back and glare at that world over my manuscript and say: "So! You thought me small, petty, obsessed with rank and etiquette, a paper soldier, a cardboard duke — oh, yes, you did, I've had my eyes on you! — but what you never comprehended was that form and substance cannot be separated and that when you gave up the former, as in your greed, your laziness and your subservience to the king and his ministers you did, you lost the other! Yes! The king squeezed you dry. Like a sponge!"

And by the time, if ever, that these memoirs are read, it will be seen that what I have said is true. And if they are never read, they will still be true, for they and I will have existed together in a moment of truth. Sometimes I have wondered if Versailles had a reality outside my pages, and my pages a reality outside Versailles. But put the two together, and there has to be something, whether my Versailles be an illusion or my work be unread. Somehow the link between them must have something to do with fact. Such, anyway, has been my faith.

And that is why I have labored to set down the pageant of the palace, day by day, season by season. I wanted my readers in the future to be able to imagine themselves in the great gallery or in the Oeil de Boeuf, or at the *coucher* or *lever* of the king. As it is impossible to tell what details of our daily life will survive into the future, it has been necessary, even at the risk of boring some readers, to set down the seemingly trivial details.

It might seem to my generation, for example, that no schoolchild of the future could fail to have heard about Louis XIV, or Madame de Maintenon, or the maréchal de Villars, or the comte de Pontchartrain. But have I not heard a young niece of my wife's confuse

Louise de la Vallière with Madame de Montespan? And did not another describe Philippe V of Spain as a Hapsburg? No, one cannot exaggerate the rapid eclipse of the past for the young. I even sometimes wonder if the reputation of the sovereign whom we like to call the "Sun King" will not depend, in some part at least, on the survival of my leather chest.

But there was still something else behind my labors. Yes, I would not have worked all those years just for posterity, or even just for the joy of writing, or even, as I say, for a life of my own. No, my memoirs have been also a kind of guarantee of sanity. When I felt that I had not fathomed the characters of those who were nearest and dearest to me — my mother, my wife, my closest friends — when I felt myself alone in a world populated by different species — different from each other, different from me — then I could make sense out of madness only by setting down persons and events in some kind of sequential chain. Or perhaps I set them down to see if I could discover such a chain. If there were no apparent order, or even truth, might not this at least be revealed in my pages?

And now that my memoirs are finished, I find that I cannot bear the loss of my occupation in writing them. I find that I always have more to say, that I must go on and on. So what I propose to myself now to do is to isolate from my gross material the events that I think have most borne on my writing of the memoirs. It seems to me that if there has been one guiding principle in my life, it has been the search for virtue: virtue in men, virtue in France, virtue in the history of France. My belief in the existence of such virtue has survived the most grievous disillusionments. Some of these have been almost sharp enough to induce me to abandon the memoirs, unless it could be argued that it was precisely such disillusionments that have most ordained their continuance. If virtue is threatened, if virtue is said not to exist, can it not be saved, or even brought into existence, by a writing that contains *all* of one man's passion for it?

And so I have decided that what I should do now is to make a record of the thing that above all else I had resolved to keep out of my memoirs — namely, myself. By that I mean myself as a mixed bag of emotions and contradictions, of fears and ideals and irritations. Of course, I already figure prominently in my memoirs — how could I not have? — but I tend to appear in them only as an observer and analyst. I am never ill, for example, unless illness is necessary to explain an absence. I am never angry, except where anger is required by some outrageous social pretension. I am never a man in love, except insofar as my marriage is a necessary part of my post of observer. But now I am going to allow myself to be more personal. I am going to allow myself to write about the duc de Saint-Simon writing his memoirs.

And *why* he wrote them.

You see, reader (if you exist), that I suffer from considerable confusion. I say I wrote my memoirs to live. That I wrote them to teach. That I wrote them to save my sanity. That I wrote them to prove that virtue exists! You will have to resolve the true answer for yourself.

2

I KNOW just where I want to begin. I want to begin with my first major disillusionment at court, which occurred when the duc de Chartres was made to marry the king's bastard daughter. But before starting on this it may be well if I said something about my own domestic life, which constituted, in my mind anyway, so sharp a contrast to the looseness of the court.

Let me start with my wife, which means that I am really starting with my mother.

My father died in 1693, when he was eighty-six and I but eighteen. As the only child of my widowed mother I took for granted that I would be precious to her, that I would supply her not only with the love and devotion that every woman must have but with the guidance and protection that a helpless female must look for in court. Mother and I had not only our château, La Ferté, in Normandy and the estate in Poitou; we had the *hôtel* in Paris and the smaller one in Versailles, necessary for the increasing hours of attendance at court on which the king set such store. We had a number of sources of revenue, but payments were irregular and we had a large number of dependents and many incidental expenses. We should indeed have been constantly hard up without expert management, and I did not see how I was to handle it all and still serve in the army in the Flanders and German campaigns.

It was at this point in my life that I came to learn the true steel of my mother's character. She made it entirely clear that she had no need or desire for a separate establishment and that she would be happy to administer my properties and run my households, even after my marriage, an event which she seemed most anxious to promote. She suggested that I, as a duke-peer, should occupy the Versailles house and that she would stay on in Paris. When I pointed out that the Paris hôtel was many times as large and as splendid as the modest edifice in Versailles, she asked me point blank if I wanted her to live in a shack!

Mother got her way in everything, even after I married. My wife very wisely made the point that letting her occupy the larger quarters, whether in town or country, was a small price to pay for not having her under the same roof. I was a bit startled that Gabrielle should put the matter quite so bluntly, but I soon came to appreciate her point of view. Mother was perfectly agreeable — so long as she got whatever she wanted. That may sound obvious, but it's not. I have known plenty of women, including the great Madame de Maintenon, the king's morganatic spouse, who are capable of being bad-tempered even when everything is going their way. So I had Gabrielle to thank for a modus vivendi that worked very well for Mother and ourselves for four decades. We paid a lot for it, but we got what we had bargained for: domestic peace.

I suppose Mother's trouble was that she had no spontaneous maternal warmth. Or perhaps I was not the child to inspire it. She had never had much feeling, beyond respect and duty, for a husband so much older than herself, and she had accepted his demise with grave composure. Her happiness consisted in careful housekeeping, rigid supervision of servants, and gossip. She was always so serious, so flat and direct in her perceptions and curiosities, so deliberate and dry in her manner, that it was sometimes difficult, seeing her with her lady friends, not to suppose that they were discussing matters of theological or political import. But coming within earshot one always found the subject the same: the latest and most highly seasoned bit of court scandal straight from the great gallery. But I must not be too hard on her, for she has provided me with much raw material.

Mother probably felt guilty about not caring more for me, which may have been one of the reasons that she labored so long and carefully in arranging a proper match. She made lists of eligible young ladies, their dowries and other assets, and was always careful to note any liabilities, such as bodily defects, bad temper or inherited insanity. When the eldest Mademoiselle de Lorges was in question, she was sufficiently enthusiastic to do enough research to rebut one presumption against her.

"The maréchale de Lorges doesn't like Gabrielle!" she exclaimed to me. "Doesn't like her own daughter! Apparently she has a passion for the younger sister. I suppose Gabrielle doesn't flatter her, the way the little one undoubtedly does. More to her credit, if so. They say Gabrielle has a good head on her shoulders, which ought to be a help to you at court. Of course, you never can tell what may happen to their characters once they're free of the convent, but at least she *seems* sensible."

I had a bit the feeling that Mother was looking for a responsible person to whom she could hand me over, in exchange, so to speak, for what the lawyers call a "receipt and release." The donor of the bridegroom would be discharged of liability when her account had been rendered. Was there not some mild contempt for our sex implied in such an attitude? Let them go, these silly men, about their silly ways, with their big hats and plumes and wigs, their bowing and scraping and their idiotic wars, and leave the "real" world to the wives and mothers! Except this particular mother was going to retire as a parent. It was high time, she evidently believed, that she should have a little fun. A woman owed herself something, after all.

Mother handled the negotiations with the duc and duchesse de Lorges herself, but she kept me abreast of them, reviewing the figures of the dowry discussions with me every night after her meeting with my hard-bargaining future in-laws. I was anxious to see my bride, and it was arranged that she should be sent back from the convent for a visit to her parents at their hôtel in Versailles.

I was at once delighted with Gabrielle's appearance and manner. She was a touch taller than I, but that I knew I had to expect in any fine young woman, and I was determined not to marry a girl shorter than myself and perhaps sire a race of dwarfs, like the Condés. She was very pale, with perfect, regular features and raven-black hair. She spoke little and modestly. I was more than satisfied.

As I was leaving the house, however, Mademoiselle de Lorges' governess followed me out and asked me in a hurried whisper if I would step into the grounds by a side door. Astonished, I nonetheless complied and found myself in a small rose garden, again facing my bride-to-be. She seemed stiff and tense, but somehow not afraid. The governess moved discreetly out of earshot.

"You will think me very bold, sir, and no doubt I am, but circumstances force me. I made up my mind this morning that I would appeal to you alone if I should decide at our meeting that you were a good man. I know that I am young and have had no experience with men, but I still think I can tell a good man."

"If you can tell that, Mademoiselle, you should be a great force at court. They know how to hide their goodness there!"

"Pray don't laugh at me, sir. The matter I must broach to you is much too serious. It is life and death to me."

I saw now, staring into those steady green-gray eyes, that this was not a girl to play flirting games with. I conformed my countenance to hers.

"Tell me what the matter is, Mademoiselle."

"My mother wishes me to take the veil. She wants to add my dowry to my sister's. She hopes, with the doubled amount, that my sister may make the greatest match in France."

I could not help wondering, even at such a moment, what Madame de Lorges might consider that to be. "A prince of the blood? Would she fly so high?"

Mademoiselle de Lorges seemed at first faintly surprised at my question. Then she shrugged. "I don't know what her imagination aspires to. But she has always preferred my sister. She has never cared for me. I don't mind that. But she should not thrust me into a convent!"

"You have no vocation?"

"None whatever. It would be torment. A living death."

"But, my dear young lady, she cannot force you! Your father would never allow it."

"You do not know my mother. She is quite relentless in getting what she wants. She would make my life unbearable. She would keep me from marrying by haggling over the dowry or hinting that I had some defect that might keep me from bearing children. My father is good to me, but he cares about peace in his household. He would not hold out against her."

"But if he knew you had no vocation! If you told him what you have just told me!"

"My mother would persuade him that I was simply hysterical. I have an aunt who is the abbess of the convent where she wishes to send me. I have heard Mother tell my father what a pleasant life it would be. 'So safe and comfortable!' she exclaims. 'With such good food and such dear, gentle friends. And one is always somebody when one is the abbess's niece. Oh, believe me, Gabrielle will do very well there. I sometimes wonder if *I* should not have been happier in a convent!' "

As Gabrielle imitated her mother's tone, I fancied that I was hearing Madame de Lorges herself. It was a perfect rendition of a worldly woman's hypocritical yearning for the cloister. Yet I wonder if even then it did not occur to me that a girl who could so perfectly ape her formidable parent might have a will that even such a parent could not have broken.

"Tell me what I can do," I said simply.

"Take me with the smaller dowry that my father is offering! I promise you that you will never regret it. A good wife can be a help at court. I have heard that from people who must know. I am sure that I can learn how it is done. And I shall place your career before anyone and anything. Please, sir. Try me!"

There was something in her tone that brought instant conviction.

Then and there I made the most important decision of my life.

"I should be proud to take you, Mademoiselle, with no dowry at all!"

Her eyes shot me a little golden gleam of gratitude, and she clasped her hands in a gesture of thanks. "Thank you, sir. From my heart. But you will not be so tried. There will be a dowry."

I had a hard time with Mother over its amount. She insisted that the Lorges were bluffing, and I dared not tell her about the scene in the rose garden for fear that she would consider the girl too brash and bold, qualities that are quickly deplored by strong-minded women when they find them in their juniors. So I simply told her that I had fallen hopelessly in love at first sight, which was in part the truth. As this was perfectly consistent with Mother's conception of the giddiness and inconsequence of men, particularly in her own family, she decided to accept it. It might, after all, have proved too difficult to plant my affections in new territory if she had had first to uproot them in old. She had a private conversation with Gabrielle, the gist of which was never revealed to me, and then, quite abruptly, agreed to the lesser dowry. My marriage contract was signed by the king and by half the royal family, and my real life began.

3

———————◆———————

IT WAS the greatest fun, introducing Gabrielle to court life and watching the glitter of the huge palace with its silver furniture and thousands of gaudy occupants reflected in the dark eyes of this soberly observing girl, who had hardly known anything previously beyond the walls and gardens of her convent. She took in everything; I had only to tell her any fact once. I could not make out at first whether this was because Versailles had made so deep an impression upon her or simply because she was intelligent. It was probably both. She was certainly never blinded by the glittering spectacle of the court. She learned etiquette as one might learn a trade.

I was up early to attend the king's lever, and Gabrielle would join me in the great gallery as he passed through on his way to mass. We made our calls on those who had apartments in the palace in the morning, sometimes separately and sometimes together. I would attend the king's dinner at one, where he ate alone at table, and in the afternoon Gabrielle would return to our little house while I followed the royal hunt, unless we both joined the king's promenade in the gardens. In the evenings there were always receptions, with card games or dancing, and we both attended the king's supper, where he sat flanked by members of the royal family. Then Gabrielle would go home, and I usually stayed for the coucher.

Our day was really a kind of celebration of the natural functions of our magnificent sexagenarian monarch: his waking, his washing, his eating, his exercising, his retiring, even his defecating. It was no coincidence that the far-flung alleys and drives around the château were all centered, in one huge geometrical design, on the royal bedroom, even the royal bed, the source of our kings. We had become so accustomed to a monarch who took so utterly for granted that his every act should be a public ceremony and who never altered the perfect regularity of his habits, that we were surprised to learn of kings in other courts who were sometimes bored or fatigued and who created distant retreats for their private pleasures.

Gabrielle was impressed with the king's endurance.

"He must have the strength of an ox," she observed to me.

"Easily. And it helps him to have been king so long."

"Can he even remember a time when he wasn't?"

"Oh, I think so. His memory is perfect, and he was at least four when Louis XIII died. His father is said to have asked him what his name was, and he replied: 'Louis XIV.' 'Not quite yet,' the dying man is supposed to have murmured."

"I'm sure it happened," Gabrielle half-whispered, curtseying deeply as the great perruque and the large aquiline nose appeared in the doorway at the end of the gallery.

She learned the thirty-four duke-peers and their order of precedence. She learned the false claims of the Rochefoucaulds to be numbered thirteenth, ahead of the Saint-Simons. She learned who was entitled to an armchair and who to a tabouret, or stool, in the presence of a son of France, and how long a train a duchess wore in mourning a prince of the blood. She learned who was entitled to drive into the Cour du Marbre and who had to descend at the main gate; what gentlemen could remain covered in the king's presence, and for whom both wings of a double door had to be flung open. She learned that the dauphin was always referred to simply as "Monseigneur," and the king's brother, the duc d'Orléans, as "Monsieur." She learned that Madame de Maintenon ranked in court only as a marquise, but that in her own apartments she was treated like a queen. And, above all, she learned about the bastards.

"There are five of these who have been 'legitimated,'" I instructed her, making no effort to control the natural disdain of my tone. "There is the king's daughter by Vallière, who is now the dowager princesse de Conti. Then there are the four by Madame de Montespan: the duchesse de Bourbon, who is known as 'Madame la Duchesse,' and her unmarried sister, Mademoiselle de Blois. And two sons: the duc du Maine and the comte de Toulouse."

Gabrielle pondered this a moment. "But if they've been legitimated, should you still call them bastards?"

"The king can make a bastard. Only God can unmake one."

We were standing at the far side of the *parterre d'eau*. Looking east now we could see the whole great shimmering yellow-white façade of the seemingly infinite palace. "You would think that the man who could build all that . . . !" She paused.

"Could do anything he wants?" I finished for her. "That's precisely what it's designed to make you think."

"And was it unlawful for the king to make Maine a duke?"

"No," I replied, wincing at this. "That, alas, was within his power. He can make anyone a peer. But what *was* unlawful was his placing Maine and Toulouse ahead of the other peers. He could not properly alter the precedence."

"But if he could make his sons peers, could he not have made them princes of the blood? And wouldn't *that* have put them lawfully ahead of you?"

"The only way the king can make a prince of the blood is in bed with his lawful spouse. A prince of the blood is a very carefully defined person. He must be a descendant, in a direct male line, from Hugues Capet, who reigned seven hundred years ago."

"Let me see if I can name them," said my good little student, holding up a hand to count fingers. "They are the king himself, of course, and his son and three grandsons, his brother and nephew . . ."

"To be exact, those are not princes of the blood," I corrected her. "The dauphin and his children are sons of France. And 'Monsieur,' the king's brother, duc d'Orléans, as a child of Louis XIII, is, of course, also a son of France. Chartres, *his* son, ranks as a grandson of France. The princes of the blood today are the Bourbon-Condés and the Bourbon-Contis, but they have to go all the way back to Saint Louis in the male line to find their first royal ancestor!" I was now almost solemn, as befitted the gravity of the topic.

"But suppose they were all to die out? Sons and grandsons of France and princes of the blood?"

"Then the peers, after seeking divine guidance, would select another first family. I presume they would start with the Uzès, who are the premier dukes."

"But wouldn't even a 'legitimated' bastard of the king, in such an emergency, have a better claim than some completely unrelated duke?"

Scandalized by this idea, I was about to reprove her, when I reminded myself that she was simply trying to learn. I was silent for a few moments until I had regained my calm. "In a Christian society," I told her, as we now walked slowly on, "we must be regulated by the sacraments. The king is our master, but no more so than God is his. He must be subject to the divine constitution. If he is to be free to promote his illicit seed to the throne, we have no more dignity than did the slaves of Attila. There have to be things a man will stand up for and die for, or life is not worth living."

"But of course I see that, dear!" Gabrielle exclaimed with sudden warmth. "I *want* to believe in the things you believe in. It's just that I have to understand them first. My father, you see, taught me that the king was everything."

"The king is a great deal," I conceded. "But he is not everything. And he shouldn't wish to be. And if he would only listen to his peers and not to his middle-class lawyer-ministers, he wouldn't!"

We saw now approaching us a cortège of courtiers following the great wheeled sedan-chair of Madame de Maintenon, drawn by two porters. Walking slowly beside it was the king himself. He was showing his wife the latest changes in the garden. When he raised his hand, an usher would tell the porters to halt. He would then tap on the glass, which the occupant would lower, and he would lean down to explain the removal of a statue or the creation of a fountain. It was remarkable to see the mightiest monarch in Christendom stooping to whisper his views through a slit in the window to a lady who was probably not even listening.

"Let us join the group," Gabrielle whispered to me. "It doesn't look well to be so apart."

* * *

Little by little Gabrielle came to be acquainted with the persons whose names and ranks she had so carefully conned. I took her one morning to call on the king's oldest bastard daughter by the Montespan, the duchesse de Bourbon, known in court as "Madame la Duchesse," in her great apartment in the south wing. Madame la Duchesse was certainly not a particular friend of mine, but she was intimate with her husband's brother-in-law, the prince de Conti, my hero, and I cultivated her for his sake.

"I certainly congratulate you on your choice, Monsieur de Saint-Simon!" the duchess said, snapping her dark, mocking eyes at Gabrielle. "We had no idea that you had an eye so sensitive to pulchritude. We feared you might bring us some little brown bride from the provinces and tell us that she was descended from Julius Caesar. But this is better. Oh, this is very fine!"

Madame la Duchesse had inherited the Mortemart liveliness from her mother. She was small and dark-haired and tense, with jet-black eyes that seemed to pierce every shield, every bluff. She said harsh and witty things in a charming way, and she never seemed to lose her temper. She was supposed to be heartless, but never wantonly unkind. She would stab you in the back only if she had to.

"Do you ever miss the convent, my dear?" she asked Gabrielle, with a smile that made her question a spoof.

"I wish I could say I did," my wife replied gravely. I was beginning to learn that Gabrielle was never shy, simply muted. "It might indicate a state of grace."

"We come to court from the convent, and some of us return. Mademoiselle de la Vallière returned."

"What was left for her, when she lost your father's favor?"

"Very prettily replied. Your wife will go far, Saint-Simon. Keep an eye on her!"

And she laughed the silvery laugh of the Mortemarts. There was a bit of a jeer in it.

Afterwards Gabrielle said to me, "She may be a bastard, but she has charm."

"I suppose there's no reason a bastard shouldn't have charm. Her mother was the most fascinating woman in France."

"And her husband is a prince of the blood?"

"Her husband is the *first* prince of the blood."

"How did he relish being married to a bastard?"

"Very little. But he was young, and did what he was told. His grandfather, the great Condé, had been a rebel and wanted to make his peace with the king. Besides, there was a precedent. His cousin, the late prince de Conti, was married off to the king's bastard by Vallière, Marie-Anne."

"It sounds as if the whole royal family was being bastardized."

"It just about is. Or will be, if the king goes through with his plan of marrying Mademoiselle de Blois to the duc de Chartres."

"To his own nephew?"

"To his own nephew."

"A grandson of France?"

Gabrielle had learned her lessons well. I patted her hand. "Even so. We may live to see the dauphin's sons not spared."

Gabrielle seemed pensive. "I should like to ask you something," she said at last. "Something personal."

"Isn't that a wife's right?"

"You must be the judge of that. And please tell me if I'm over-stepping myself. I have been noting the principal activities of the men at court. They hunt. They gamble. They seek positions. And then . . ." She hesitated.

"They make love?" I finished for her, with a wink. "All except me. I have no need to go beyond my own blissful nest for that."

Gabrielle smiled, perhaps the least bit perfunctorily. "But the other things — you don't go in for them, either. You never gamble. When you go riding, it's by yourself or with Savonne. And there doesn't seem to be any office you're after."

"There isn't. I have everything I want."

"Well, that's just it. It occurs to me that as a courtier . . . you're . . ."

"Unique?"

"Well, let us say highly individual. I cannot help wondering why you would not prefer to be at La Ferté."

It may seem strange to my reader, but until that moment I had never really asked myself that question. I was so full of the life at court that I perhaps may have wondered if life really existed anywhere else, or at least with anything like the same intensity. To be a part of the king's ritual seemed as important as saying mass was to a priest. To live close to the source of power struck me, perhaps fantastically, as a kind of accomplishment in itself. If heaven, as some maintained, was simply the contemplation of God, perhaps the contemplation of the monarch was a kind of earthly preparation for it. I said this now to Gabrielle.

"But you're so critical of the king," she objected.

"Of the man, for he *is* a man. And he has failings, grave ones. He has allowed himself to be persuaded by parvenu ministers, who have no sense of Old France, that his power is unlimited. But for the *office* of the monarch my admiration is complete."

"Well . . . shouldn't you, then . . . shouldn't you . . . ?"

"What?"

"*Do* something about it?"

I stared. "Do what about what?"

"Help to advise the king where he is going wrong. Couldn't you seek a post?"

"Beauvillier is the only peer he has ever had in his cabinet."

"I see. Well, of course, I know nothing about it."

Gabrielle, with her perfect tact, seeing that I was upset, dropped the subject and did not raise it again. But she had given me something to think about. Why indeed could I not bring my influence, however small, to bear on the turn of events? I had a sharp eye, an excellent memory and a readily recording pen; I had many friends and connections in court, some in the very highest places. Was it necessary to be a prince, a general or even a minister to have a hand in the shaping of events? Did I have to look further than Madame de Maintenon to see in what devious ways power could be exercised?

Gabrielle had to give up court life shortly after this colloquy because of a painful and difficult pregnancy. She was very much disturbed at not being able to be with me at Versailles, but she rightly considered it her more vital duty to deliver a healthy heir, and she forced herself to spend long tedious hours on a couch. In the end, alas, all of this did little good, for not only was she brought to bed prematurely of a girl, but of a dwarfish and defective one. My disappointment, however, was obliterated by the passion of hers.

"I've failed you! I've failed you!" she cried again and again, twisting her thin arms tightly about my neck. "But you'll see! I'll produce an heir for you. You will not have saved me in vain. Oh, I *promise* you, dear one!"

My mother and I feared for her life, so desperate was her frenzy. I had had no conception of the violence of her gratitude to me and the intensity of her compulsion to make good. I was almost awed at the passionate loyalty of this ally I had brought into my life, like a man who walks with a savage dog that regards all the world as threatening his master. But Gabrielle's fit subsided at last, and she was once again the quiet, patient, reserved and observing creature that she had been. Only she never showed any interest in our poor little girl.

4

GABRIELLE's first substantial contribution to my career at
court was in the affair of the alms bag. It was the custom
after mass for the young duchesse de Bourgogne, the king's granddaughter-in-law, who, as we had lost both queen and dauphine,
was the first lady of France, to ask a duchess to pass a velvet purse
for contributions to the church. The "Lorrainers," members of the
House of Guise, who should have ranked with us as peers, were
always claiming a higher position as "foreign princes," based on
silly titles bestowed on them by the Holy Roman Emperor because
of scraps of land held along the border. I now learned the latest
outrage: that their ladies were claiming exemption from the alms-
bag duty. There was nothing for me to do but organize the dukes
to make a similar claim.

"But who will pass the alms bag?" Gabrielle asked me.

"How should I know? Perhaps some simple gentlewoman."

"But if the duchess *asks* me?"

"If she asks you, of course, you must. But she can't ask you if
you're not there. What I'm saying is that the duchesses should ab-
stain from mass."

"Won't it anger the king?"

"I can't help that, my dear. It's the Lorrainers he should be mad
at. They've been an infernal nuisance ever since the days of the
League. Why a monarch who's so sensitive to treason should put
up with them, I can't conceive."

Gabrielle, I had to admit, was correct about the king's reaction. After the first day, when half the duchesses at court absented themselves from mass, the duc de Beauvillier sent for me, and Gabrielle and I went at once to his apartment in the north wing. The duke, who, as I have indicated, was the only peer in the king's council, was an old friend of my parents and had been my guide and mentor ever since I first came to court. I admired him without reserve and had even once offered to marry any one of his eight daughters. Fortunately for me and Gabrielle, the oldest had wished to take holy orders, the second had been a cripple and the rest too young.

"I think you ought to know," Beauvillier told me, "that the king spoke of you this morning at the end of the council. He said that ever since you had resigned your commission, you have been obsessed with petty questions of rank and precedence."

"Oh, he remembered about my commission?" I had left the army, two years before, to devote myself to the court.

"The king remembers everything."

"Then I wish he would remember the countless disloyalties of the Lorrainers!"

"If he doesn't appear to, you can be sure he has a reason. In any case, he wishes me to convey to you his desire that the duchesse de Saint-Simon should pass the alms bag on Monday."

I hesitated. "Is that an order, sir?"

"Is the king's desire not always an order?"

"Very well. But surely I need not be present. He will not require me to assist at my own humiliation?"

"That is up to you."

"Ah, but, my dear, may *I* make a suggestion?"

I turned to Gabrielle in mild surprise. It was not like her to intervene in my conversation with an older person. "Certainly."

"Request an audience with the king! Tell him you raised the issue of the alms bag only because you thought it was one in which he was not concerned. But now that you know he wants me to carry the bag, you are not only proud but honored!"

I looked into her anxious eyes with even greater surprise. Then I turned to the old duke.

"Do it, Saint-Simon!" he exclaimed with a laugh. "And be thankful for a smart little wife."

"And then ask the king for an apartment in the palace!" Gabrielle hurriedly added.

"Speak to him at his dinner," Beauvillier advised me. "Request an audience for tomorrow. I'll put in a word for you at the coucher." He glanced at his watch. "It's almost one now. Hurry up if you want a spot near his table!"

* * *

The king liked to sup with members of his family, but he was inclined to dine alone, that is, alone at table. There was always a group of courtiers standing by the small table at which he was served, silently regarding him. He ate, as he did everything else, with remarkable solemnity, dignity and grace. He would raise a chicken bone to his lips, take an incisive, effective bite and then chew slowly, his dark, glazed eyes focused in an opaque stare. When he turned his head to survey the room or the watching crowd, this stare might be softened to encompass not an acknowledgment, certainly not a greeting, but simply a recognition. Somehow you always knew that he knew you. And he not only knew who was present; he knew who was not.

There was something hypnotic about the effect of one man exercising a natural function while his audience remained motionless. It was like watching a priest take communion. The huge, high-piled black perruque moved rhythmically with the royal mastications; the high, arched brows twitched; the great aquiline nose snorted after the thick lips had sipped wine. His most ordinary acts were majestical. Those of his household who were privileged to watch him on his closed stool said that he made even his defecations imperial.

It was permissible for those standing closest to the table to address the king when he was not actually swallowing or masticating. Waiting until his gaze took me in, I stepped forward and bowed.

"May I be permitted a word, sire, on the question of the alms bag?"

The dark eyes emitted a faint glitter. "There *is* no question, sir. The matter has been regulated."

"But, sire, I humbly suggest there has been a misapprehension of my attitude. I wish only to make explicit my utter loyalty and devotion."

"Very well, then. When you wish."

He turned to his goblet, and I stepped quickly back. So far, so good. After the dinner Beauvillier told me exactly what to do next. I should stand in the front row of the courtiers waiting outside the council chamber the following morning and step immediately forward when the king came out. He would then appoint a time for an audience, perhaps immediately. It was all simple enough, but nonetheless I hardly closed my eyes that night, and Gabrielle made me drink two glasses of wine with breakfast.

At noon, outside the council chamber, I did as I had been told. The king paused to give me one of his glacial stares, a mixture of surprise and faint irritation. Then he must have recollected what Beauvillier had told him at the coucher, for, beckoning me to follow him, he stepped into the embrasure of a window, where he folded his arms and waited for me to speak.

I began with what I had intended to be the very briefest summary of the alms-bag controversy, but he interrupted me testily.

"I have no time, sir, for such nit-picking. You spend your life fussing over imagined slights. You had far better have stayed in the army, where you were of some use."

I saw at once that the situation was desperate. I even dared now to raise my voice.

"I had no intention, sire, of bringing up the issue of ducal rights. I only wish to tell you that, as a duke, my sole aim is to be of service to you. Had the duchesse de Saint-Simon and I known in the beginning that it was your desire that she should pass the alms bag, she would have passed it joyfully, and with my total blessing, among the humblest in the land, in the most fetid of hospitals, in the darkest of dungeons!"

The king's countenance at last relaxed. "Now that's talking," he said in a milder tone.

I went on, carried away by my excitement, to declaim on my loyalty and that of my ancestors; to tell him that we were second to none in our zeal for the royal service. The king let me continue in this way for what must have been several minutes before interrupting me at last by raising his hand. And then, to my astonishment, it was to answer me in a tone that was almost benign!

At first, I hardly took in what he was saying. His effect on me was hypnotic. I kept my gaze so firmly fixed upon his lips, not presuming to look him in the eye, that soon I began to feel a bit dizzy. His opening and closing orifice conjured up in my fantasy the mouth of a cave in the middle of a desert of infinite range and emptiness. It was as if no life could be contained in the parching dryness; that only in the darkness behind that agitated adit could there exist sustenance and support. But how could one make the passage past those teeth with any hope of safety? I was hearing the king, a voice kept saying to me! I was actually hearing the king!

And then the purport of his words began again to come through to me. His tone was almost avuncular.

"I had not thought, sir, that you had a proper excuse for quitting the army. However, if you truly wish to be of service here at court, there will always be occasion. But let me give a piece of advice. You must watch that tongue of yours! It is too inclined to be free. If you take care of that, *I* shall take care of you. I do not forget that my father loved yours."

This reference to my beloved progenitor completely undid me. The tears, I am not ashamed to admit, started to my eyes, and I proceeded to pour forth my gratitude. I do not recall everything I said, but I know that I must have expressed with passion my desire to serve him in all matters. I ended by begging to be considered for any rooms in the château that might be available so that I should have more ample opportunity to pay my court. The reader, in another era, may smile, but he will not be able to imagine the effect of Louis XIV on his subjects when he chose to be gracious.

He spoke again. "I shall keep your request in mind." That measured tone always convinced the petitioner that his plea had been securely filed. "One never knows when a vacancy may occur."

And then, with that brief though definite, courteous though irrevocable nod, he moved on to the great gallery. I could feel in the very air of the chamber around me the soaring of my reputation.

Gabrielle met me in the antechamber with the round window known as the Oeil de Boeuf and took in at a glance the success of my audience. When she heard about the apartment, she clapped her hands.

"That means we're sure to get one!"

Indeed, she was right, for we were granted an apartment of three tiny rooms the very next day. They were hardly comfortable, yet they were more coveted than the greatest mansion. For only by living *in* Versailles could one fully appreciate the delights of the court. The palace at night had its peculiar pleasures and opportunities. The public was evicted, and the royal family retired behind closed doors, guarded by sleepy Swiss sentries. Something almost like informality prevailed.

It was a time for small, intimate suppers or conversations, for passionate post mortems of the day's events: who was in, who out, who had said what to Madame de Maintenon, who had been alone with the king. It was a time to call on the ministers and perhaps catch them, relaxed, in indiscretions. Oh, yes, an apartment was a great boon, and I was properly grateful to my wife.

"Now you've got everything you need!" she exclaimed proudly when we at last surveyed our redecorated reception chamber. I had even hung my father's portrait of the beloved Louis XIII over the little marble mantel.

"Need for what?"
"For whatever you want."
"And what do I want?"
"Ah, my dear, *you* must provide the answer to that!"

5

THE VIDAME DE SAVONNE, at this period of my life, was my
closest friend. He was the merriest person imaginable, when
he was not the gloomiest, for his changes of mood were dramatic.
His popping blue eyes, curly blond hair and cauliflower face could
be like a clown's when he roared with laughter, but when the
melancholy mood descended, he seemed more like a drowned
puppy. Yet up or down, he was always the most loyal of friends.
He had a charming way of seeming to need me, both in prosperity
and when winds blew ill.

It is commonly said that even men who have the courage of
demons on the battlefield may show as cravens in the gilded salon,
but I never fully believed it until I became intimate with Savonne.
I saw him lead a cavalry charge at Neerwinden with a recklessness
that was almost reprehensible, yet I have also watched him trem-
ble so violently before Madame de Maintenon, who was a cousin
of his mother's, that he could hardly articulate a sentence. He professed to hold as sacred as I the rights of the peers, yet he was constantly betrayed by the weakness inherent in his affable and con-
ciliatory nature into intimacies with just the sort of parvenus who
most threatened our ancient prerogatives. When I accused him of
being light minded, he would shrug and retort that "favor was
everything" or "money ruled the roost," seeming to suggest that
the fashionable was also the inevitable, and that resistance had
gone out with the ancient martyrs.

And then, too, he laughed too much. I have always noticed that the man who tells you that he could part with anything but his sense of humor usually lacks one. Well, Savonne never said that, but he could be counted on to burst into shrieks of laughter at all the silliest things in court. He did not do so in a way to hurt peoples' feelings. On the contrary, he was very careful to wait until he was with a "safe" group before exploding. But he took too much pleasure in the ludicrous. It was more than a distraction; it became an evasion. Look around any court at your really great men, and you will find that two out of three have no sense of humor at all. It is not a necessary tool for the ambitious. Interpret everything men say in joke literally, and more than half the time you will hit their true meaning.

Savonne was always influenced by my example, at times too much so. I was disconcerted that he resigned his commission when I did. In the first place, he had much greater aptitude as an officer; in the second, being still unmarried and more than averagely susceptible to the attractions of wine and women, he was a constant prey to the temptations of court life. However, he assured me that he was determined to be steady.

"I shall model myself on the duc de la Rochefoucauld," he said. "I shall be the perfect courtier!"

Rochefoucauld was so assiduous in his attendance to the king, never missing a lever or a coucher, that he was reputed to have slept only three nights outside a royal château in twenty years.

"But what is it you wish to obtain?" I inquired.

"Anything there is to obtain!" he exclaimed, throwing up his hands. "In Versailles, if you're not busy getting something, you're busy losing what you've got."

I had to admit there was some truth in that. Had not Gabrielle made almost the same point? There were times when the courtiers reminded me of my pack of beagles at La Ferté waiting for the daily ration of meat to be flung to them. But Savonne's first real enthusiasm at Versailles turned out to be just the opposite of what this interchange had led me to anticipate. He showed distinct signs of becoming more devout, and I do not mean just the kind of devoutness that Madame de Maintenon had made fashionable. It was again, I suppose, his tendency to extremes.

He was, as I have said, a cousin of Madame de Maintenon, and as she was always benevolent to her relatives, no matter how distant, he had occasional access to the rooms from which the venerable morganatic spouse of our august sovereign dominated the whole of the great palace, if not indeed the whole of Europe. It was here that the king, usually accompanied by a minister, was inclined to spend his evenings: he in his armchair, she in a kind of armless sedan-chair whose red curtains protected her from drafts, on either side of a small table covered with state papers. But it was not all work. Majesty would sometimes retire with his elderly partner for the rites of love, which she, by all reports (nearing seventy as she was!), found the source of scant enjoyment.

At the point at which I write, Madame Guyon, the mystic or fake, depending on which side one took, was high in the favor of the mighty marquise, and my credulous friend was soon taken in by her, dazzled to be included in the select company which gathered to hear her in afternoon séances at Madame de Maintenon's when the king was hunting.

"You should come with me once," Savonne told me enthusiastically. "It's an extraordinary experience. Here I am in the heart of mammon, perhaps the very earthiest spot in the whole earth, and what do I find? A holy of holies! We know that God is everywhere, but somehow one hadn't expected to run into him at court!"

This was decidedly distasteful to me. Unlike Savonne, I had no desire to talk about my religious experiences. I kept them strictly to myself. I went into regular retreats at Father La Trappe's monastery near La Ferté, and I found it necessary to my happiness to believe that God should exist and that spiritual union with him should be the ultimate goal of our being. But in some curious fashion it did not suit me to believe that God was at Versailles —

except, of course, in the chapel. Versailles, as Savonne suggested, was the world, matter, the earth. It had to be just the opposite of the spirit.

"If I may say so without furiously offending you," I observed acidly, "your distinguished cousin is a consummate hypocrite. Molière caught her to the life in *Tartuffe*. I don't know anything about this Guyon woman, but I suggest she's made out of a patch of one of the Maintenon's black gowns."

"You think you're so original!" Savonne retorted. "And all you do is repeat what everyone says about poor Cousin Françoise. They fawn on her in public and then blast her behind her back. But if she's a hypocrite, I'd like to know what she gets out of it. Do you think she couldn't have anything in France for the asking? You know she could! And what does she spend her life doing? Running her convent school at Saint-Cyr, interviewing clerics, regulating church matters, dispensing charity. Where are her palaces, her diamonds, her golden coaches? If she's being a hypocrite about the simple life she must be an idiot, and nobody's ever called her *that!*"

I had to admit his point was well taken. Why should a woman with her power and position try to please anyone but herself? But there was still an answer, though perhaps too subtle a one for my friend: Madame de Maintenon was trying to fool God. She had conquered this world, and heaven offered her new territory. It was perfectly true that she lacked the jewels or robes of a queen, and her official position in court ranked her below the princes of the blood and the peers. She was supreme only in her own exiguous apartment. But there she *was* supreme; there she could scold the king's daughters until they emerged red-eyed, and summon to her presence the greatest in the land, who would drop everything as soon as they saw her usher. No, Savonne could not see it, but *I* could: that to glide in to the king's supper, soberly garbed, and take her place at table below some chit of a duchess while everyone greeted her entrance with silent reverence could have created a finer ecstasy in her soul than to have joined the king on his silver throne in the great gallery! Oh, yes, the old trot was a gourmet in the delights of power as well as in those of religion. Not for her the vulgarity of display or the loneliness of true prayer. Never has "simplicity" been more worldly.

Gabrielle, who had been present at our argument, now took Savonne's side with respect to his original suggestion.

"I think we *should* go to Madame de Maintenon's," she urged me. "You like to know everything that's going on. Perhaps some great religious movement will emanate from her séances. Besides, it's considered a great privilege to be asked."

Well, that was certainly true, and with Gabrielle's voice to spur on my own insatiable curiosity, I found myself succumbing. It was indeed a signal honor that Savonne should have been allowed to bring me to Madame de Maintenon's at all. The reputation that I had achieved for being a stickler in matters of rank had not endeared me to a woman whose principal aim in life was to promote the king's bastards, the blindly adoring governess of whom she had once been. We agreed to go with Savonne to her rooms at the next séance.

"We are glad to hear that you are taking an interest in spiritual matters, Monsieur de Saint-Simon," the Maintenon greeted me as I entered. "We had thought of you as more terrestrially minded."

"It is my desire to conform in all matters to the king's taste," I replied with a bow. "And we know we follow that when we have the honor to be here."

Madame de Maintenon glanced at me suspiciously, but then nodded, deciding to accept the compliment. She was certainly an attractive woman. She had clear pale skin, like marble, without a wrinkle, and large penetrating dark eyes. She was dressed, as usual, in black velvet, which wonderfully set off her pallor and dignity, with no ornaments but a large jeweled cross, which hung on a chain, a gift of the king. Her voice was soft and sweet but very firm, and she moved her arms and head gracefully but with determination. She was a bit too much the manager; it was even possible to imagine her as the keeper of some great inn, smiling, gracious, but with keys jangling at her waist and a mind that could embrace the change of linen as well as the reception of a monarch. I always wondered that the man who had tired of the infinite charm and variety of the Montespan could be satisfied with anyone as cool as her successor. But there was no accounting for tastes in love, particularly after a certain age.

There were some dozen persons in the room, mostly ladies, and Madame Guyon now proceeded to discourse for an hour on the doctrine of grace: who was possessed of it, who was not, who was saved, who damned. It was all a kind of half-baked, fashionable Jansenism. She was the most irritating kind of mystic: a woman whose downcast eyes, pursed lips and gentle tone expressed her merciful condescension towards the sinners with whom her hard lot had cast her. She was the perfect companion for the Maintenon, a proper acolyte in her smug little temple of hypocrisy. Even the awe created by the latter's presence could not restrain my argumentativeness. When the lecture was over and those of us who dared were permitted to question the oracle, I promptly did so.

"You imply, Madame, that it is already determined which of us are saved and which damned?"

"Yes, and irrevocably, sir," came the sweet reply. "For if God knows everything, as he must, he knows the future."

"Then he has no choice in the matter? Having once made up his mind, he cannot change it?"

"God does not have a mind, in our limited sense of the word. God is everything."

"And would everything not include a mind?"

"It would include a mind and no mind. It would include a changeable mind and an unchangeable one."

"I'm afraid that's a bit beyond me."

Madame de Maintenon intervened. "Who are you to understand such mysteries, Monsieur de Saint-Simon?" Her tone was that of a governess to a child whose good conduct could not be relied on. "Very little is revealed to the wisest among us, let alone young men at court."

"I am the humblest of the humble, Madame," I replied respectfully. "I only seek illumination."

"We have heard about your humility, sir. You want everyone to know your exact rung on the social ladder."

"One can be humble and still know one's place on that ladder, Madame. One's exact place." Was there the hint of a glare behind her sharp glance at me? Did she pick up a reference to her own equivocal position? At any rate, she said nothing. I turned again to the Guyon: "What I cannot comprehend is why, if we are already saved or damned, it does one any good to be good. Or even to pray."

"How like a man to ask that!" Madame Guyon explained, directing a sad little smile towards the Maintenon. "As if we needed a reward for doing good or for praying! As if that were not the only way to true happiness! There can be no bliss comparable to communion with God. No true joy in this life save in the contemplation of the next!"

"But surely that cannot be if the next is hell fire," I protested. "Or do you mean that God grants communion to those he has damned? That he offers a short respite of bliss to those who face an eternity of punishment?"

This brought our sovereign's morganatic spouse back into the discussion like a ship of the line preparing a broadside. "And if he *does*, sir, is it not evidence of his mercy? Or are you so addicted to the pleasures of this world that you have lost all sense of awe?"

At this point Savonne intervened desperately to protest that he would not be associated with my questions, and the topic was changed. I sat there, silent and fuming. It was really intolerable to contemplate what old Maintenon had got away with. It was not enough for her to have risen from a hovel in Martinique to the lap of the minor nobility, from being widow of a crippled, scatological poet to spouse of the king — oh, no! She had to have, in addition to the delights of contemplating heaven for herself, the delights of contemplating the rest of us in hell. And yet no thunderbolt was ever to strike the old bawd. She would die in peace in her bed at St.-Cyr at the age of eighty-four.

An usher appeared in the doorway. It was the signal that the king had left the council chamber and was approaching. We all at once arose and took our leave. On the stairway to the terrace Savonne reproached me angrily.

"How could you be so impertinent? I can never take you there again."

I paused to eye him coldly until Gabrielle, walking ahead, was out of earshot. "I should think there might be some shit that even you couldn't eat."

Gabrielle, hearing Savonne's retorting exclamation, turned back to us.

"My dear," she reproached me mildly, "I fear you went too far."

"Tell him, Gabrielle, tell him! He thinks he knows everything!" And Savonne, with this parting shot, stomped off.

"But don't you think I had a point?" I demanded of Gabrielle.

"Oh, I know nothing about that. I was referring only to your irritating Madame de Maintenon."

"What about God? Don't you think the Guyon may have irritated *him*? Deciding for him whom he damns and whom he doesn't?"

Gabrielle seemed to consider this for the first time. "I really don't know. I hadn't thought of it."

Something in her tone made me curious. "Do you know something, Gabrielle? I've never heard you express an opinion on a religious matter. Is it possible that you don't . . . *believe?*"

She gazed calmly back at my now graver expression. "I suppose I believe in God. But he's still the god who runs the convent that Mother wanted to lock me up in."

"But that's heresy!"

"Then let's keep it between you and me. I don't want to be burned." She smiled, but her eyes did not. "*You* are my god," she said in a sharper tone. "That's why I want you to be somebody!"

6

*D*ECIDEDLY, I was beginning to feel pushed by my wife. At times I resented this and would go through pouting days when I hardly spoke to her. But at others it would begin to seem to me that without the impetus that she provided I should have been destined to vegetate uselessly all my life at court.

If I was going to embrace a cause or a project, it might as well be a great one. If I were to be hanged, let it be for a sheep. I regarded the promotion of the bastards to their intermediate rank between the princes of the blood and the peers as the gravest existing threat to the established order under which we lived. I was convinced (with absolute justification, as it turned out) that the male bastards would ultimately be declared capable of succeeding to the crown. Very well. I should start there. What would be the king's next step? To marry Mademoiselle de Blois to his nephew? I would work to prevent it.

It was at this point that I needed a powerful ally, and who was more fit than my court hero, the prince de Conti? He was a prince of the blood, head of the house of Bourbon-Conti, a gallant warrior and a brilliant man, whom the king kept dangling idly in court because of the horrid contrast Conti had offered on the battlefield to the king's poltroon bastard, Maine. Furthermore, Conti was safe from a bastardly alliance, as he was already married to his cousin, one of the Condés and a sister of Monsieur le Duc. He was also, be it admitted at once, the lover of Madame la Duchesse, but this fact played no part in my plans. One could be the lover of a bastard without approving of bastardy. And not only was he an expert in genealogies and questions of precedence; he was an ardent believer in the restoration of the rights and duties of the peers. Here was a prince who offered a gleam of hope in our benighted days!

Furthermore, he was not only my hero; he *looked* like a hero. He was, to put it simply, the most attractive man in the whole court, adored by men and women alike. He had very pale skin and black shiny ringleted hair, which he wore unpowdered. He was slight but muscular, and, though inclined to tenseness, moved with ease and agility. His eyes were large and dark and moist, and he spoke with a sweetness that made one at first suspect him of flattery. Yet why should he have stooped to flatter anyone? He simply loved people, and delighted to please them.

The reader should not gather from this that he was indiscriminate. On the contrary, he could be very keenly observant and would often make the most devastating remarks in the gentlest of tones. And he was fearless, too, quite undaunted by the rank or power of the person whom he might be criticizing. Of course, his station in life made it impossible for him to fight duels, but he had proved his courage over and over again on the battlefield, where he had exposed himself almost as recklessly as Savonne in cavalry charges. He seemed, indeed, to enjoy danger.

His popularity in the army had made him odious to the king, so Conti in the past year had been kept away from the military at court, where he had taken his revenge by carrying on his flagrant affair with Madame la Duchesse, to the unconcealed fury of their much less attractive spouses, who were, of course, brother and sister to each other.

Conti was always kind to younger people at court, and I used to call at his beautiful rooms in the south wing, which looked over the orangerie. He had a collection of Poussin's Roman landscapes and some remarkable Cellini figurines. One of these, a nude youth, seemed as perfectly made as himself. He liked to quiz me on questions of precedence, and he would gaze at me, while I answered, with that mild fixed stare of his. Sometimes I wondered if the velvet tone in which he made his comments was not mocking me. This was particularly so on the afternoon when I told him of the affair of the alms bag.

"It would be a comfort if we could look to you as our leader in these disputes," I suggested.

"As your master of etiquette?"

"I hope you don't think I underestimate you!"

"No, no, my friend." His fingers grazed my arm. "But for one who has dreamed of a generalship . . . well, surely you understand. In my brain I hear the roar of the cannon . . . and in my ears the chink of the alms bag."

"But one goes with the other," I protested. "I, too, have heard the cannon . . ."

"And without flinching. I saw you at Neerwinden."

I flushed with pleasure. "Ah, sir, if you had your rights in the army, we should fear no enemy. I was saying to my friend Savonne only this morning: thank God for your marriage. You are safe from the bastards! The blood of the princesse de Conti is as pure as your own."

"Purer," he retorted, with another of his smiles. "*I* don't forget that my mother was Mazarin's niece. I'm sure *you* don't."

I returned his smile discreetly. Of course I didn't. "Many royal houses have been happy to marry into the families of cardinals," I replied tactfully. "In Italy it has always been a badge of honor."

"Well, at least Mazarin's nieces were legitimate. They were not like 'papal nieces.' And basically I agree with you about our sovereign's bastards. I cannot but feel how we must look to the eyes of Europe when the 'most Christian king' makes princes and princesses out of the issue of his adulteries." Here, quite suddenly, he winked at me. "Charming as those princesses may be."

"Let us concede that one of them at least is the most charming woman in France," I said with a bow to acknowledge his liaison. "Excepting of course our spouses."

"Excepting them, of course. But has it never occurred to you, my friend, that the whole business may be a scheme? Not just the elevation of the bastards, but all the games we play here at court?"

"Games?"

"Well, take this question of the alms bag. You think you're defending an important right of the dukes, do you not?"

"Only because it's a question of persistent encroachment. The particular issue must always seem trivial. But each bit of territory lost is lost forever."

"Ah, but is there any territory really left? Isn't *that* the basic question? Isn't the fuss over the alms bag really designed to make *both* the Lorrainers and the dukes think they have something to fight over?"

I stared. "You mean the king *designed* it that way?"

He laughed. "Oh, I don't say he's that clever. It's simply the way the system works. It keeps us all here, chained up in this great gilded palace, like children playing with dolls."

"You mean our cause is lost? Hopelessly lost? Is that what you're trying to tell me?"

"Let's put it that I merely face the possibility."

"So there's no point in my offering the smallest resistance? Let the king satisfy his bastards with other peoples' honors?"

"They will find he is playing the same game with them that he has with others. He takes a privilege; he yields a bauble."

"And what will be the end of it all?"

"An absolute monarch looming grimly through a cloud of butterflies. Lovely butterflies!" Conti laughed as he flicked the lace on his cuffs. "Or has it happened already?"

I was desperate. Images rushed through my mind. I thought of my father's wise, sad countenance. I remembered his story of how the saintly Louis XIII had rallied our forces against the Spanish invaders when even his iron cardinal had crumpled in panic. I saw our cavalry at Neerwinden. I saw the writhing, the dying. I turned now to face the mocking despair in Conti's eyes.

"I said that every issue had to be trivial!" I cried. "It's not so. There *is* one great one before us. Will you stand by and allow your cousin Chartres to be married to Mademoiselle de Blois? Will you see a grandson of France wed to the king's bantling?"

"My dear fellow, what can I do?"

"You can talk to Chartres. I'll go with you. He looks up to you. He admires you greatly. Oh, he's told me so! We can stiffen him!"

Conti seemed to consider this. A shadow passed across his face. "Poor Chartres, he doesn't deserve it. He's really a fine young fellow, you know. People don't understand him, because he's shy and blunt. Well, what can we lose?" He shrugged his shoulders. "The king hates me, anyway."

"Because you showed up what a coward Maine is!"

"Perhaps just a bit, by contrast. But who wouldn't be a hero compared to poor Maine?" Here he burst into his high laugh. "But I never intended it, so help me!"

I returned stubbornly to my point. "Will you go with me and talk to Chartres?"

"You really think it will do any good?"

"I think there's a chance. Monsieur is very proud of his blood. He can hardly relish seeing his own son wed to a bastard. If Chartres puts up a fight, Monsieur may take his side. And I wonder if the king will really cross his only brother in a matter so dear to him."

Conti seemed to weigh all this. "How does the Chevalier stand on this?"

The Chevalier de Lorraine, sinister character, was the damned soul of Monsieur.

"He may have promised the king his help in getting Monsieur's consent in return for supporting the Lorrainers in the alms-bag matter."

"Then it'll be a tough one." Yet Conti looked up at me now with his bright smile. "Why should we fear a tough one? Can it be tougher than Neerwinden? Saint-Simon, I'm your man!"

It was agreed that we should go into Paris the very next day and see Chartres at the Palais-royal. Conti permitted me to enlist Savonne in our cause. I was much excited, but when I told Gabrielle that night, I was surprised at her silence. I forgot everything, however, when she told me that she was pregnant again.

7

*P*HILIPPE, DUC DE CHARTRES, only son of Monsieur and only nephew of the king, was just my age, and he and I had known each other since childhood. Chartres had in common with his older cousin Conti a great attraction for women, but it was almost the only quality they shared. He was stocky, muscular, crude and outspoken. He was not handsome, but he had good eyes, which fixed you with a faintly sneering but not altogether unfriendly challenge. "What's your game?" he seemed to be asking. "What's there in this for you? Oh, come now, you must have a game. I know *I* do." He was afraid of nobody but of his funny little father and of his uncle. He loved to drink and to womanize, and, as he was too independent to make any secret of his disorderly life, he was in constant bad odor at court, which, in turn, reintensified his natural rebelliousness.

He came to Versailles rarely and passed most of his time in the immense Palais-royal, which Richelieu had built for himself and bequeathed to the crown. This edifice was the scene of widely varying entertainments. Chartres would give dinner parties (I was never invited nor did I wish to be) behind closed doors, where the servants would retire after leaving the meal and the wines, and where every sort of debauch would then take place. Monsieur, on the other hand, an unabashed homosexual (the only one, be it added, whom the king tolerated), and his lifelong crony, the Chevalier de Lorraine, held gatherings in which beautiful young men, not always of proper pedigree, predominated. "Madame," a big, hefty, plain-spoken German princess, who was as much of a man as her husband was a woman, preferred to spend her time at Versailles. I think she was in love with her royal brother-in-law, but the poor old cow-bull would never have had a chance with him, even in the pre-Maintenon days.

When Conti, Savonne and I called at the Palais-royal, we were ushered into the great gallery that Richelieu had hung with the portraits of those who, in his opinion, had made France great. I remember it as a somewhat curious selection, ranging from Dunois to Jeanne d'Arc to Louis XI to Bayard, and ending, of course, with Richelieu. We did not at first perceive Chartres, who was sitting at the far end, but as soon as he saw us, he jumped up.

"They're going to make me marry her!" he exclaimed. "They're going to make me marry the bastard!"

"Your father hasn't consented?" I cried in dismay.

"No, but he will. The Chevalier will make him. The Chevalier will do anything for money, and Father will do anything for him."

"Then you must refuse!"

"That's all very well for you to say, Saint-Simon. But would you have refused *your* father?"

"If he'd asked me to marry a bastard? Yes! It is probably the only thing I would have refused him. I'd have cut my throat had he bade me to. But to make a match so degrading . . . never! And I'm not a grandson of France!"

"Conti's brother didn't worry about it," Chartres pointed out sullenly, glancing at his cousin, who had turned to the great portrait of Richelieu by Philippe de Champaigne. "*He* was the one who started the fashion."

"Ah, but he died of the shame of it," Conti replied, without turning his gaze from the great cardinal. "He is a sorry precedent to cite. I wonder what old Hawkeye here would have said. I think he would have kept the royal blood pure. Look at the history in this gallery! The men who made France great. Guesclin, Montfort,

Bayard, Dunois, look at them all, nobles and warriors. Why, the room seems to throb with the muffled sound of their tramping feet! Surely they would not have bowed to the spawn of Montespan and Vallière!"

Had the mocking note disappeared from Conti's velvet tone? Was I making a fool of myself in thinking that I could detect even a faint tremor of something like passion in it, passion that he had always professed to consider as not in the best of taste in a society that worshiped the superficial, a society he both deplored and enjoyed? He walked several paces down the gallery and paused before Jeanne d'Arc. "I suppose if this dear lady were alive today she'd ask for the rank of foreign princess, like our silly Lorraine friends. But she lived in a nobler time." He turned now and walked deliberately back to Chartres. "Believe me, cousin," he said in his gentlest tone, "your father will bless you for your disobedience. Nobody cares for our blood more than Monsieur. Nobody has cared more for the prestige of our house. To see his only son misallied might be as fatal to him as a bad marriage was to my brother. He may give in to the king out of momentary weakness, but he will repent of it later. And then how he will cherish you for standing out!"

The double doors at the end of the gallery were now flung open, as is done only for a son of France, and we stiffened to attention. Monsieur came briskly in, his high heels clicking on the parquet. He was a fantastic combination of inconsistencies: dignity and effeminacy; authority and coyness; serenity and nerves. His head, with the huge black perruque, beady eyes and large, aquiline, Medicean nose, rose from a mass of ruff, ribbons and diamonds like an owl's above a messy nest. The Chevalier, who followed him, had a boy's face at sixty, a handsome boy's face, but there was something tight and sinister about that unlined skin. One felt it might suddenly crack, like an aged apple.

"Have I interrupted you young people in some naughty project?" Monsieur demanded, looking with a malignant gleam from one to the other of us. "I trust my disreputable son is not leading you gentlemen into trouble? You, too, Savonne? Beware of him!"

"On the contrary, Monsieur, I'm afraid I was boring these young men with a lecture in history," Conti replied, indicating the Champaigne portrait. "I was holding forth on the domestic policies of the great cardinal."

"A very capable man. But people exaggerate his accomplishments. They give him credit for everything that was done in my father's reign."

"May I take the liberty of saying how passionately I agree with your royal highness!" I burst out. "I have always regarded Louis XIII as the greatest of our monarchs! I learned it at my father's knee."

Monsieur cackled merrily. "Don't let my brother catch you saying so! But it's all right, Saint-Simon. Your father was a good man and a loyal friend. He told me some funny stories about the cardinal. Do you know that when Richelieu lived here, he used to have apoplectic fits? Oh, dear, yes! He would imagine he was a horse and run up and down the corridors, whinnying and stamping. Such a scandal! The palace would have to be shut up tight. But people *would* talk. You do your father credit, Saint-Simon. I am sure he would be happy to know that you are so well married and settled." Here he sighed and glanced at his son. "Would that we could say the same of my boy here."

"I shall be happy to marry, father, any lady whom *you* select."

"Whom *I* select?" Monsieur glanced briefly at the Chevalier, who remained impassive. It was obvious to the five of us that Chartres was implying that, left to himself, without fear of the king, or the Chevalier, his father would never pick a bastard for a daughter-in-law. "And just what do you mean by your emphasis, sir? Do I detect an impertinence?"

"None whatever. I simply meant that — blindfolded if you will — I shall be happy to take the hand of any woman in Europe who represents your own choice."

"Would that not be any woman whom your father *named?*" the Chevalier put in, with a sneer in his tone.

"My father is not the head of his family," Chartres replied impassively.

"That will be enough, my boy," Monsieur said testily. "I think you *are* on the verge of impertinence. Is he not, Conti? We shall cut him off at this point before he dabbles with treason." Monsieur, with a snort, turned his attention to Conti. "Tell me, cousin, how you select your pages. You have the handsomest at court. The Chevalier and I were talking about it as we came through the courtyard. We heard you were here, so we looked for your livery. And, of course, there it was, on a *beauty!* We paused to have a little chat with him. Such a clever young fellow. So devoted to *you,* cousin."

As Conti merely bowed in silence, Monsieur turned again to me. He did me the honor to lead me aside for a word in private.

"Don't get too mixed up with my boy and his parties, Saint-Simon. You've still got a reputation to lose. But if you would care to come to one of my little gatherings here, very select, you know, you would be welcome."

We chattered on this way, he increasingly friendly, I circumlocutory, elaborately polite, for though I had no wish to be associated with the inmates of the Palais-royal, neither did I want to arouse the ire of a touchy prince. I knew that his taste was for boys, but as I was smaller than average and young-looking for my age, I was by no means sure of being exempted from Monsieur's favored classification, and indeed his civilities that day were very warm.

I made my exit as best I could and joined Conti and Savonne in the courtyard. Before getting into his carriage, the former turned to give me a brief warning.

"Watch out. The Chevalier has his eye on us. Old Maintenon will know in an hour that we've spoken against the marriage."

8

Conti was right. In less than a week's time I felt a chill in the atmosphere at court. My old friend, the duc de Beauvillier, told me that the king had again spoken unfavorably of my resigning my commission and had cited the sorry effect of my example on Savonne. And when the latter presented himself at Madame de Maintenon's he was informed that he would not be received. When he told me this, much shocked and chagrined, I decided to ask Gabrielle if she could find out anything. She was to spend the afternoon at the apartments of "Madame," the duchesse d'Orléans, playing cards, and I waited in the vestibule until she came out. When she did so, I took her for a stroll to the Basin of Latona, where she confirmed that I was in the bad books of the Maintenon. Madame, who was passionately opposed to her son's marriage to the bastard, had as good as told her so.

"She said you were in *her* good books, anyway," Gabrielle added. "Not that that does us much good. Poor lady, nobody listens to her."

"But everyone's against the marriage!" I exclaimed indignantly.

"Yes, but they don't *do* anything about it. And then there's this business about Madame Guyon. Did you know she's been sent to the Bastille?"

"My God, no! Why?"

"The king's confessor has persuaded him that she's a Jansenist, and she's shut up until a clerical commission can study the case. Of course, Madame de Maintenon dropped her like a hot potato as soon as she picked up the first whiff of her ill favor."

I whistled. "So *that*'s why poor Savonne found her doors shut. It seems a bit hard, considering that he only met the Guyon through her."

"No, Madame de Maintenon is perfectly consistent. Anyone who met the Guyon *only* in her apartment is all right. But Savonne met her twice more — at the duchesse du Lude's — *after* the wind had changed."

"I see. These are the distinctions on which our lives depend! But I think I had better somehow explain Savonne's innocence to the king." I paused, but Gabrielle said nothing. "Don't you think the king should know *how* Savonne got into this?"

"Suppose you speak to Monsieur."

"Monsieur?"

"If Savonne is really in trouble, it's not over Madame Guyon. It's over the marriage. What I think you should do is give Monsieur a hint of the price you're all paying. He likes you. And he has to be basically on your side about the marriage. He can't object to your wanting a proper match for his own son, even if the king forces him to consent to this one. So, if we lose, and Chartres has to marry Mademoiselle de Blois, he can make your peace with the king."

I had to admit that this was shrewd, even if it struck me as a bit ignoble to make personal plans for shelter in the event of the wreck of a noble scheme.

"But Monsieur's so volatile," I objected. "Everything depends on who's last been with him. And where."

"Where?"

I placed a protective arm about her waist. "Ah, my innocent, we mustn't peek too closely into the private life of our sovereign's brother."

But my wife's demure little smile did not in the least convey the innocence that I had assumed. "You mean what Chartres refers to as 'Papa's little weakness'?"

"Oh, you know."

"Is it not a loyal wife's duty to know what goes on in court?"

I sighed. "I suppose so. But I hate to have your pure little mind contaminated with such filth."

"My 'pure little mind' can take in worse than that. Be sure when you go to Monsieur that the Chevalier is not with him."

I arched my eyebrows. "Do you think it's safe for me to be alone with Monsieur?"

Gabrielle's smile showed a new sophistication, of which I could not quite approve. "Oh, I guess you can take care of yourself."

"Even against the fluttering hands of royalty? I can hardly knock down a son of France."

But she continued to smile as if we were consciously playing a scene. "A loyal subject must suffer many things," she said demurely. "I'm sure there's a dispensation under the circumstances."

Something tore in my heart, and the sky seemed as suddenly dark as if the clouds had been pulled shut by frantic hands.

"You mean that I should . . . should . . . !" I paused, gasping.

"I meant nothing at all," she said quickly.

"But you did!" I almost shouted. "You think I should let Monsieur bugger me!"

My wife paled, and her eyes flashed as I had never seen them flash. "Sir!"

What could I say? What could I do but apologize? For a few minutes I thought I must have offended her so deeply that there could never again be a question of true intimacy between us. And, then, in another flash, I saw that I was forgiven. Yet it struck me that Gabrielle's quick return to her normal demeanor of self-containment might mean that she had not been really upset at all, that she took these things for granted and that I, poor ninny, was just someone to be discreetly handled. And if *that* were so, how could she truly love me? Did she regard me as a task to be performed, the usual silly ass of a husband that a helpless girl found herself married off to, one who had to be cajoled and manipulated so that she and her children might rise in the world and not be buried in the avalanche induced by his blindness? Did I not know about those cynical mothers who warned their daughters in the cradle about the "myths" of honor that men so crazily cared about?

Gabrielle now proceeded to make matters even worse. She tried to relieve our tension with a silly anecdote. She told me that Imbert de Torrence had solved his problem with Monsieur by letting it be known at St.-Cloud that he had a contagious skin disease!

At this, I left her without a word. I found myself walking down the Royal Alley to the Canal, and from there into the woods. When I turned back at last it was beginning to be dark. As I came out of the forest it occurred to me for a moment that I was lost, but then through the trees I caught the glint of water and realized that I was near the edge of the Canal at the bottom of the "green carpet." As I approached the Basin of Apollo and then started to circle it, I had a curious sensation of being drawn along by the marble border. It was as if some long tentacle of Le Nôtre's landscape gardening had reached out to recapture me from the tangled wilderness and was now handing me to another tentacle, and then another, so that I was lifted from alley to alley, across grassy swards and graveled paths, up steps, past fountains and over terraces, the patterns becoming more meshed, more rigid, more complicated as I proceeded, until I was delivered safely back to the heart of the great palace itself.

I did not see Gabrielle at the *jeu du roi*. She had gone to our rooms. But I knew now what I had to do for Savonne. After the supper, I stepped boldly forward, as the king rose, to show that I requested a word. What was my dismay to meet the full glare of the royal countenance in terrible anger!

"You quit my service, and now you wish to run my court! That will do, sir! I have nothing to say to you!"

He moved on, and I stepped quickly back. But the place that I had occupied might have been scooped out of an iceberg. I felt all around me at once the mortal chill of my disfavor.

9

THE DAYS that followed only confirmed my disgrace. It was an appalling experience to be out of favor with the king at Versailles. You saw it reflected in everybody's behavior, from the way your valet handed you your blouse to the way Madame de Maintenon looked through you as she passed you coming out of chapel. Some of it might have been your imagination, but most of it was not. For Versailles was the king's home as well as his palace; his moods quickly permeated its hundreds of galleries and apartments. We were like schoolchildren under a strict headmaster whose presence was felt everywhere.

Savonne, too, was in trouble, and I advised him to get out of court and go to his mother's in Anjou until the Guyon affair blew over. I even found that I could sense a difference in the attitude of so staunch an old friend as the duc de Beauvillier. He advised me to re-apply for my old commission!

What turned my disgrace, however, from a bleak desert to what was almost a verdant garden was Gabrielle's attitude. It was as if she welcomed it as a chance to make up for having shocked me. A man must have an ally if he is not to perish in the void of royal disfavor. The feeling of being utterly alone, a bell without a clapper surrounded by noise, a single current running against the ocean, can be unbearable. But if there is a hand to squeeze your own, an arm to be slipped under yours, a sympathetic murmur in your ear, you can face the world. Gabrielle seemed to have waited for adversity to show what her true mettle was.

"Of course we're going to the reception tonight! Do you want people to think you're cowed?"

Never a word about the fatal consequences of my failing to heed her advice! Never a syllable about my unjust indignation! Almost simultaneously with my first doubts about Gabrielle came the flood tide of my reassurance. I was actually a happy man in the crowded rooms that night.

Chartres was there, brooding as usual. I joined him in his corner and asked if there was any news about his marriage.

"I had a talk with my 'bride' today," he replied with a sneer. "Or rather she 'received' me, at Madame de Maintenon's. For don't think for a minute, Saint-Simon, that Mademoiselle de Blois shares your low opinion of her origin. She believes that the child of majesty outranks a mere nephew."

"Even a lawful nephew?" I demanded. It angered me that even a chit of a girl should also reason so absurdly. "Even a grandson of France? And does she consider that she greatly honors you in offering you a mother-in-law who was not married to her father?"

"Oh, we never speak these days of Madame de Montespan," he said with a jeering laugh. "We have nothing as vulgar as a mother. We sprang from the brain of Zeus, like Athena!"

"I suppose it's Madame de Maintenon who has taught her such arrogance."

"Well, if you've got to be a bastard, you may as well be an arrogant one. And speaking of arrogance, I hear that Madame la Duchesse is giving Conti the devil of a time."

"Why?"

"Because he took my side!"

I stared at him in surprise. "I thought she didn't care about her sister."

"She may not. But when it comes right down to it, those bastards always stick together." Chartres now laughed so loudly and crudely that several persons standing nearby glanced around. "Can't you see poor Conti, snatching a quick one between the jeu du roi and the supper, huffing and puffing away, in terror that Monsieur le Duc may barge in and catch them at it? And all the while his mistress of the marble skin, her lovely thighs twisted around his torso, is murmuring in honeyed tones how nice it would be if her baby sister married a real prince!" Here he stamped on the floor with a snort of disgust as his mood changed. "And we men are crazy enough to think these little cunts care about us!"

"Please, someone may hear you!"

"And Savonne has taken to his heels. And you're in the king's shit house! Let's hope, anyway, if worse comes to worst, that the little Blois has as luscious an ass as they say her big sister has!"

Chartres had a way of thrusting his sexuality into his discourse with men as if to reduce the world around him to a stable of rutting horses where he was the major stallion. There was something undeniably attractive in his very coarseness, a masculinity that rode contemptuously over rank, precedence and Godliness; a rude way of stating that grandson of France or no, prick for prick, he was your equal and very likely your superior. I could not approve of his atheism or of his morals or even of his tolerance of immorality in others, but I never had the smallest doubt about his honesty. Chartres was fundamentally on the side of the angels.

"Let us trust that you never have to make that discovery," I rejoined.

"Anyway," he exclaimed, hitting me on the back, "it might be a way of screwing the king!"

10

_I_ DECIDED to discuss these developments with Conti, and hearing, the next morning, that he was hunting the boar with the dauphin at Meudon, I rode out there. I arrived late for the hunt, but soon caught up with the stragglers, and I found Conti riding alone across a pasture. He reined up to let me come abreast of him. The hounds, he explained, had lost the scent for the third time, and he was bored.

I asked him if he thought that Savonne's trouble could possibly have any relation to the Guyon business. He shook his head.

"No, no, it has to be the marriage. There's no doubt about it. One of my pages quit me. He went, you may not be surprised to hear, to the Palais-royal." Conti cantered ahead suddenly as he said this. I followed, admiring his perfect seat. He and his horse might have been a centaur.

"I suppose he will find life there more amusing," I remarked with a smirk as I came abreast of him again. "Is he the one Monsieur so admired?"

"He is. And the worst kind of gossip, too."

"Well, what can he gossip about?"

"What do you _think_ he can gossip about, Saint-Simon?"

Conti pulled up his mare and gave me an odd look. There was a seeming defiance in it, yet also a kind of shyness, and perhaps something of an appeal. As I pulled up and stared back at him, in what was now a constrained silence, it seemed to me that this appeal might have been articulated as: "Oh, come now, haven't you ever been tempted . . . and, if not, can't you sympathize . . . haven't you any *imagination?*" He spurred his horse and cantered ahead again. I picked up my reins and followed.

"Sir!" I cried, but he kept right on going.

For some ten minutes I must have ridden across country behind him, my thoughts in a tumble. I even wondered if I should not go home and consult Gabrielle about the mores of my own sex. For if she knew all about Monsieur and his minions, perhaps she could tell me how it was that a man who enjoyed the favors of the most dazzling and (by all reports) the most demanding woman in court could have the inclination, or even the energy, to dally with page boys. I had always abominated the "Italian" vice. Yet somehow its grip on a man as attractive as Conti seemed to put matters in a different light.

But *why* should that be, I asked myself hotly, unless I had no morals at all?

We trotted now, and I endeavored to pull my thoughts together with some coherence. After all, the vice was widespread. Had not even the sainted Louis XIII been accused of it? My father used strenuously to deny this, but a man as upright as Beauvillier had told me himself that *his* father had once found young Cinq-Mars naked in the king's chamber when he had burst in with an important military dispatch. Perhaps it was simply a Bourbon trait. Or might it have been that Conti was so attracted to beauty in human beings that he had to pay tribute to it in whichever sex it appeared? But what kind of a question was *that?*

I reined up for a moment and let Conti get farther ahead. My pulses were throbbing, and I felt my tongue thick and dry in my mouth. Was it conceivable that *I* was attracted by the vision of Conti with a pretty page? Where was my advocacy of the prince taking me? No, no, this had to be madness. I was simply putting as good a frame as I could around an odious picture. Conti was an exceptional man, a peerless soldier, a great prince. Nothing that he did could be really odious, for the simple reason that he brought so much charm to the doing of it. An exception had to be made for him in my mind and heart.

Once I saw my way, I became calmer. I spurred my horse ahead and caught up with the man who was still my hero. I reminded myself of the sexual habits of Julius Caesar, of Alexander the Great, of Hadrian.

"I just want to say, sir, that nothing — nothing under the sun — can affect my high regard for you!"

He reached over to touch my shoulder. He made all his gestures exquisite. "I know you are strict in your views, so your generosity is the more appreciated." For a few moments we rode on in a silence that with any other companion would have been awkward. As it was, I felt a curious elevation of spirits. Then Conti's mood seemed suddenly to alter again. His voice, when he spoke, was grating as I had never heard it. "Do you know something, Saint-Simon? Things would have been different had I been given a command. But what in the name of Christ is a man to do when he's married off to a dwarf of a cousin and kept dancing his heels on parquet floors?"

Conti now proceeded to relate to me, as we walked our horses slowly across country, the story of his affair with the duchesse de Bourbon. It took the rest of our ride, and he had to finish it in his suite at Meudon over a bottle of wine. I have tried to put together his account as I remember it, but no doubt some of my own style will have crept in. Everything about Conti was beautiful, so my impression of the whole may have embellished the parts to something more than they were as spoken.

11

I THINK you know, Saint-Simon, that I was a special favorite of
my father's older brother, the prince de Condé, known as the
'Great Condé.' My uncle's own children were small in stature and
inept at sport, and he set great store by these things. Also, poor
creatures, they were sadly plain, and he admired good looks, even
such slight ones as your humble friend may be blessed — or
cursed — with. I was immensely proud of the hero's esteem, but
I paid a heavy price for it, first in the bitter resentment and jealousy
of my cousins, and second (and more important) in the intense
anxiety that it generated in me as to whether I could ever turn
into a soldier remotely worthy of such inflated admiration.

I made long visits as a youth to Chantilly and rode and shot with
my uncle and spent the evenings by the fire listening to him discourse on his campaigns in the Lowlands, in Spain, and in our
poor divided France of Fronde days, when he was in arms against
his own sovereign. Of course, it was not the boy king that he had
hated but my mother's uncle, the wily Mazarin, and it spoke
worlds for Condé's devotion to myself that he was able to overlook
my relationship to his villain. Still another reason that I should
have to prove my manliness in his eyes! I learned about all his
battles, all his campaigns; I studied each maneuver and tactic; I
could identify every officer in the huge dusky battle canvases that
filled the great hall. I remember that my mother, who had some of
the Mazarin nose for detrimental anecdote, used to say that it was

a regrettable touch of vanity in an otherwise great man to have included in his military gallery pictures of his defeats of the troops of his own nation. It amused her that these were signalized by the addition of the muse of history in the upper-left-hand corner veiling her eyes from the scene! But I found Mother simply irreverent. The Great Condé was to me without fault.

It has become fashionable to look back upon the age of the Fronde as one when the great nobles petulantly and childishly sacrificed the peace of the realm to their own personal bickering. We have come to see it as a time when civil war was looked upon as a kind of sport for the upper classes, when pitched battles took the place of the boar hunt, and the siege of citadels that of the chess game. All this, allegedly at the expense of the starved poor, is now contrasted unfavorably to the order and stability of our own era, when the quarrelsome peers and princes have been safely domesticated at Versailles. But I impenitently mourn those more vivid days.

Anyone, surely, would have to admit their sharper color, their acuter flavor. I never tired of hearing not only of the warriors — of Beaufort, Turenne, Villeroi, and my own father — but of the great ladies so close to the battles, sometimes actually commanding on besieged ramparts — my gallant aunt de Longueville, the intrepid duchesse de Chevreuse, and the great Mademoiselle herself, the king's cousin. I thrilled at my uncle's description of the latter, striding in scarlet equestrian habit along the parapets of the Bastille and giving the signal with her raised riding crop for the cannon to open fire on the royal troops. Corneille, I was sure, had found in these Amazons the models for his great pagan queens: Sophonisbe, Viriate, Pulchérie.

My trouble was that I came to see war, subjectively, as a kind of test of the manhood of François de Bourbon-Conti. There can be tremendous egotism in an awed and bashful boy. Mighty, menacing, glorious as these figures of my uncle's tales seemed to me, I had nonetheless a fantasy in which they existed principally as a challenge to myself. I never made the smallest connection between warfare and any benefit to a conquering, or detriment to a conquered, people. No, it existed simply to prove who were men and who were not. It was the sport of gods. It was glory, and without glory, life was a thing of baubles and ribbons, of bows and curtsies. Without glory, life was Versailles.

It was inevitable that I should choose an army career, and I shall never forget the terrified anxiety that attended my first campaign. I was literally sick with fear that I should prove a disappointment to my uncle. He was no longer, of course, on active duty. He was old, and, as it later turned out, already dying, but I knew that he had officers who would tell him of my every move, and that he looked to me to carry on the glory of his name. I was not, certainly, a good officer in that first action. Nobody can be a good officer who is more obsessed with looking brave than with defeating the enemy. But my responsibilities were fortunately few, and it did not affect the tide of battle that I was so intent on exposing myself to danger. Happily, I was noticed, not for exposure but for courage; the dispatches mentioned me, and my uncle had some slight reason to be satisfied before he closed his eyes for the last time. Another example of the grossness of my egotism was that I cared more to learn that he had died informed of my gallantry than that he had died! And yet I suppose I loved the grizzled old war horse as much as, until then, I had loved a human being.

I offer this background because it is necessary if you are to understand what happened to me when, after five years of vigorous campaigns, the king summarily removed me from the front and stationed me at Versailles. I was given no place in his council, no function in his court. My wife and I had little relationship. I had not been her choice, any more than she had been mine. She was, of course, the Great Condé's granddaughter, but even this was not a bond, for she, like most of her family, had hated him. What was I to do with my life at Versailles? I turned to cards, to women, to wine — to too much of all of them — and then, in my extremity — to the other thing. I suppose, as I had always associated court life with the effeminate, the unmanly, there was a kind of crazy logic in my crowning my activities with what I deemed the most unmanly conduct of all. It was a species of suicide.

My experiments in the "Italian" vice, however, never had the effect of weaning me from the other sex, and it was during my brief affair with Madame de Créon that I incurred the hostility of my wife's sister-in-law, the duchesse de Bourbon. The latter and I had at first respected each other's wit and taste; there had even been a time, shortly after we had both been married off to grandchildren of the Great Condé, when we had seemed to eye each other with the prospect of a still closer relationship. I had been attracted from the beginning to that diminutive vision of pale skin and raven hair and those sparkling dark eyes. But Madame la Duchesse's wit, which had been my delight on leaves from the army, began to seem too corrosive when I was forced into a life of idleness. I tended now to identify her with the king. Her father had ruined my life, and his jokes at my expense began to take on the aspect of a jeering commentary from the paternal compound. What was she but part and parcel of the whole vicious apotheosis of Louis XIV?

I was too much of a gentleman to hold her bastardy against her, but it nonetheless had the effect of linking her in my mind to the unlawfulness of much of what the king was doing. And so it took very little to bring my feelings towards her to active animosity. She objected to my intrigue with Madame de Créon because the testy officious little duc de Bourbon had an eye for that lady himself, and Madame la Duchesse encouraged his infidelities as an excuse for her own!

At the king's supper, one night, when I found myself seated by Madame la Duchesse, she turned to me with a small smirk and asked me:

"What should I call the little Créon? My lover-in-law? One needs some term like that, don't you think? We have so many new relationships in court these days."

"You might call her 'lover legitimated.'"

"Fie, prince, put back your velvet glove. That's too blunt a blow for a man of your wit."

"Your turn, then. I bare my chest. Strike!"

She looked at me as if she were searching the most vulnerable spot. "They called our grandfather-in-law the Great Condé for his conquest of enemy territory. I think we'll call you the Great Conti for your occupation of areas that are . . . shall we say, less rigorously defended?"

This bold association of my name with the female sex organ in the presence and almost within the hearing of the king would normally have made me roar with laughter. But the use of obscenity to dramatize the contrast of my present life with the glorious past of my hero made me so indignant that the tone of my response must have been actually grating.

"It's your father's fault that I live as I do! Why don't you use your influence to get me a command?"

"And be the cause of sending you away from court? Be the possible agent of some damage to those beautiful features? Ah, no, dear prince, a thousand ladies would scratch my eyes out!"

I turned away from her, too wrathful to trust my speaking tone. The king, at any rate, was about to rise, and I noted that he had observed us. Had there been a hint of disapproval in those opaque eyes at the animation of our discourse? The king, I knew, with Madame de Maintenon, tried to keep Madame la Duchesse's conduct at least outwardly respectable. He deplored in his children any activity that recalled his own lascivious past and framed in irony his present stiff morality. Any association with a man of my descending reputation would be just what he desired the least. Which was just what gave me my idea.

I would become the lover of Madame la Duchesse! It would be an exquisite combination of revenge and pleasure. I determined to set about it at once, and the very next day I presented myself at the apartment of Madame de Maintenon at a time when I knew my prey would be there.

"So, prince, you are seeking respectable company for a change!" Madame de Maintenon's tone was haughty but not unfriendly. She was always grateful to have the princes of the blood dancing attendance on her. "We are flattered. I am only sorry your dear little wife is not here. She seems to spend more and more time with her mother in Paris these days."

"She is indeed, ma'am, the very symbol of filial devotion. A saint, I venture to suggest."

"Well, we could use one in the family."

I bowed in silence, letting her "family" pass, and then went over to take a seat by Madame la Duchesse.

"What in God's name brings you here?" she challenged me at once. "Do you have the nerve to do your chasing under the very nose of the old prude? Don't forget she was once a governess!" She laughed mockingly. "And mine, too! So it can't be me you're after." She affected to glance about the room. "Which of these lovelies is it?"

"You needn't look so far."

"Oh? Is she close?"

"Do you think me so insensible to beauty?"

"You mean *me?*" She burst into another laugh. "Oh, come, prince, don't take me for a complete ass!"

"Why should hearing my suit make you that?"

"Because it's hard enough to find a lover in this court with the smallest amount of genuine affection without picking one who *starts* by disliking me!"

I looked at those flashing eyes and marveled at her candor. She did not even bother to lower her voice. We were just out of earshot of Madame de Maintenon, but almost any other woman in a position as vulnerable as hers would have at least glanced about to check on her safety.

"I don't know why you assume that I dislike you," I observed in a milder tone.

"Because you have it in for bastards!" she exclaimed. I could hardly believe my ears. Her brother, Maine, and her sister, Blois, would have had their tongues cut out rather than so much as utter that word. "Oh, don't deny it," she went on. "You think I'm like my sister. You think I consider myself above everybody because I'm the king's daughter. But I know very well what I am, and so does she, for all her airs. Do you ever stop to think what it's like to be a natural child in a palace where the favorite indoor sport is counting quarterings? Well, I'll tell you! You read the sneer behind every courtly bow, the derision behind every curtsy. The king can legitimate us till the cows come home; he can marry us off to princes of the blood; he can elevate us to the stars by decrees; but will that affect by one jot or one tittle the tranquil disdain in the eyes of a hundred little princes de Conti or ducs de Saint-Simon? You know it won't!"

I was a bit ashamed to discover that this perceptive creature should have so easily divined my hostility. Did it not prove that she had more feeling than I had hitherto suspected?

"What makes you assume that I think these things?" I asked.

"I've watched you! I watch dozens of people who never suspect it. My mother used to say that we Mortemarts were born with an eye in the back of our heads." Here she emitted another high peal of laughter. "As she has never looked back in her life, that must have been how she spotted Monsieur de Montespan's horns!"

I could do nothing better than laugh with her at this. "I wish you would let me at least be your friend. We all need friends at court."

"Friends? Pooh. What are they? You're like all the handsome men at Versailles. You have the naïveté to believe that the people whom you attract by your charm are better friends than those whom you attract by your rank. They're not. They're all the same. They all desert you at the first whiff of disgrace. What's the difference?"

"If I can't be your friend *or* your lover, what can I be?"

"My brother-in-law!" she exclaimed and turned away to talk to the Maintenon. But the smile that she gave me in parting was far from discouraging.

And so I started to pay my court to Madame la Duchesse. She received my attentions with a smiling acquiescence. She even, after a bit, professed her responding ardor, but always as if we were playing a high comedy in private theatricals. It was impossible to know what she meant. It was impossible, indeed, to know anything about her except that she was thoroughly enjoying herself. She would avow her passion to me in a perfectly normal speaking tone at the jeu du roi, and when Monsieur le Duc, small, bustling, officious, jealous, would make his hurried way across the chamber to interrupt us, she would, without a pause, without slurring a syllable, smoothly change the topic to some current bit of court gossip, just as he came up.

I at last proposed a rendez-vous. She agreed, but never appeared. The same thing happened a second, a third time. Her excuse was always perfect: her husband had suddenly turned up; a child was ill; the king had sent for her. Nonetheless, I was convinced that she was playing with me. Why else did she laugh so much? No woman who was really in love could laugh that much. Black curls, black sparkling eyes, rouged thick lips, the finest jewels in court — and that laugh — was it not all the very portrait, even a banal one, of female vanity and lightness? Everyone *knew* that Madame la Duchesse had no heart. And, of course, I was in love myself now. Well — I deserved it.

So I told her at last what I thought of her. I broke off. I vowed I was through. As I had expected, she only laughed. But then on the king's weekend at Marly, when I was occupying my pavilion alone, as my wife was visiting her brother at Chantilly, I pulled the bell chord for my valet to dress for the supper, and a strange youth came in.

"I hear you like pages!" she exclaimed with a shout of laughter.

This time I roared as loudly as she. It was all so utterly outrageous, there was nothing to do but accept it.

And then, almost immediately with the union of our bodies came the union of our hearts and minds. It was a glorious, a fantastic experience. Neither of us had ever loved anyone before. Neither of us had ever really much liked anyone before. We had been too full of ourselves, our fears, our nerves. I had had a feeling for my poor mother, yes, and I had deeply admired the Great Condé, but passion was a new thing. And she, unhappy creature, had hardly ever seen her mother as a child, and who ever loved the king but Vallière? And her husband, of course, was a toad. When we discovered each other, it was as if we had found our own private chamber in the crowded court, one with fine, clear windows overlooking gardens that nobody else could see. For that chamber was *us,* and the rest of the world, our spouses and friends and children, the king himself, were not so much unreal as outside, apart.

Oh, I do not mean, of course, that people did not know. That was the extraordinary thing about it. Everyone knew that she and I had something that nobody else at court had. It drove my wife and Monsieur le Duc wild. Even the king, I think, eyed us with a kind of envy. Our love hung in the air at Versailles, if I may wax poetical, like some glittering golden spangle, turning slowly around, iridescent, fragile. Anyone might have taken a shot at it and brought it down, but nobody did. Nobody dared. Till now.

* * *

Conti paused here. He seemed to have finished his tale.

12

"BUT WHAT can they really do to you?" I demanded of Conti, in an agony of apprehension as to what his silence foreboded. "What can they do to spoil something that belongs so peculiarly to you and her alone?"

"I haven't told you the worst. They've put my ex-page in the Bastille. They picked him up at the Palais-royal. There's the threat of an ecclesiastical commission to investigate charges of vice."

"At the Palais-royal! Why didn't they arrest the whole household?"

"Because this is only a *threat*. Like a dirty reaching hand. I had had this crazy idea that I had provided Madame la Duchesse with an oasis in her difficult and dangerous life. And now to have that dirty hand stretch out to sully her, to soil her, through her connection with a man involved with pages . . ."

"But women don't mind that, don't you know?" I interrupted warmly. "Women are much better than we in keeping things separate. Madame la Duchesse won't *care* what people say."

"She's tougher than I, you mean? I agree. Even so, I should like to make the occasions as rare as possible when she has to use her toughness. But let me put it on another ground. If the king so desires, he can use this commission in a way to discredit us all. Even Monsieur, if Monsieur won't agree to the marriage."

"But surely he won't disgrace his own brother!"

"Won't he? You don't know him. The lower the star of the family dips, the brighter his own shines alone. Oh, I don't say that he would invoke the criminal law against me or Monsieur. That wouldn't be necessary. In a vice trial we should simply be pilloried by the pointedness with which our names were omitted. Don't you remember how the poison trials ruined Madame de Montespan without her being a defendant or even a witness? I'm not dreaming this up, Saint-Simon. The Chevalier has been to see me. He's in the pay of the king, you know. Oh, he dotted his *i*'s and crossed his *t*'s! We must all accept the marriage or a judicial inquiry into the morals of the Palais-royal."

"You'll sacrifice Chartres to save your own skin!" I cried, in the misery of my disillusionment.

But Conti's patience with me was inexhaustible. "Rather to save the royal family, my friend. I'm afraid you've lost your perspective. To spare Chartres from wedding a bastard, you'd let this scandal sully us all. It doesn't make sense. I'm sorry, but we learn in warfare that there are times for strategic retreat. Chartres' marriage is the lesser of two evils. And I have told him so."

"I think I had better go back to Versailles at once." I rose, trembling in my indignation, and hurried outside to mount my horse and ride back to the château. On the way I had the chance to reflect reluctantly that there might be some merit in Conti's position. But it was still his fault to have placed himself in a position to be blackmailed! I wondered if I could ever forgive him.

When I reached the palace and had changed, I found that the king was in council, which was unusual at so late an hour. There was a rumor afloat that a special announcement was forthcoming, and the galleries were more crowded than usual. I passed Monsieur le Duc, asleep with his mouth open, on a bench near the council chamber door. Groups of two or three were strolling up and down the great gallery. To my surprise I found Chartres standing by himself in a window embrasure, looking down the Royal Alley towards the Basin of Apollo. When I came up to ask him what brought him to the château, he told me, rather curtly, without turning his head, that he had been ordered there.

"Then it's come!" I exclaimed in dismay. "Your father's given in!"

"I don't know. You've heard about Conti's page?"

"Yes, but we can survive that!"

"Can we?" He turned to me now, and I saw that his face was alive with emotion. There were actually tears in his eyes. "Don't you think my poor father has suffered enough for one lifetime? Do you know what he went through as a younger brother, Saint-Simon? He was deliberately effeminatized to make him less of a rival to the king. They introduced him to sodomites when he was twelve! Yet he was still a better soldier than the king. And when he was married to his first wife, do you know what happened? The king seduced his own sister-in-law!"

"Is that really true?" I asked, allowing my historical curiosity to get, for the moment, the better of my mission.

"He told me so himself! He's been through hell, I tell you! And he's always been the most wonderful father to me."

"Until now."

"Well, look at the pressure the poor man's under! First, the Chevalier, who hates me, and now the king, with this buggery business."

"But the king loves Monsieur. Despite you all, I can't believe he'd expose him. And, besides, if you will forgive me, sir, who doesn't know about your father's life?"

"There's all the difference in the world between a criminal trial and a spat of gossip. Monsieur would be horrified by the conviction of one of his people. It would blow to bits the little temple of fantasy in which he lives. And what about Savonne? He'll wind up in a heresy trial, if he doesn't watch out. And Conti? How will he relish the page trial? He's not known for that sort of thing, as Monsieur is. *Yet.*"

I looked him straight in the eye. "See here, sir, if you think I'm going to change my position about your marriage because of these threats, you are quite wrong. Would you like me to write to the king about it? And tell him what I and the whole court think of this marriage?"

Even Chartres gasped at this. We both looked over to a group of ladies who had entered the gallery with Madame, Chartres' mother. I saw that Gabrielle was among them. She had spotted us immediately and was watching us with her placid stare. Now she smiled as our eyes met, and I felt giddy at the thought of what I had just offered to do. It would be suicide, but a splendid one. Maybe it was time that somebody committed suicide for a principle at Versailles!

"Do you know what, Saint-Simon?" Chartres exclaimed. "I believe you're capable of it. But I'm not worth it, my friend." He gripped my shoulder. "No, truly, I'm not. And I'm not worth making my father any unhappier than he already is. I'm not worth disgracing Conti and dishing you and Savonne. Bring on the fair ass of Blois! Oh, yes, I grant, there was a moment when Conti was talking — that day in the picture gallery at the Palais-royal — when I had a dim little sense of history and my possible role in it — but it passed. Maybe it was just Conti's way of putting things. He has the devil's own charm, and plenty of eloquence, but sometimes I wonder if he really believes in anything much more than I do. I sense a kind of cousinly despair in those dark damp eyes of his. So unlike yours! *You* believe passionately in everything you say, but you don't make it charming, the way he does. I keep reacting against your thrusting people into all those little cubbyholes. Sometimes I think you and the king aren't really all that far apart. Order, order, order — like all those goddam gravel walks out there." He turned moodily back to the window.

"Never mind all that!" I exclaimed with heat. "Tell me that you won't consent to the marriage, and I'll be with you. To the end!"

I think for a moment he was moved. We exchanged a long look. And then we realized from the sudden silence around us that a royal usher had approached us from behind. As Chartres turned, the man bowed and told him that his presence was desired in the council chamber. I followed him and saw, through the open door, the figure of the king in his armchair. Beside him I made out the diamonds and ruffles of Monsieur. All was over.

History is made in small moments. Who knows what might have happened had our interchange continued? I do not think more than ten minutes elapsed before the double doors were flung open again and we heard the tapping of the royal cane.

"Ladies and gentlemen, the king!"

I closed my eyes and moved my lips in silent, agonized articulation of the anticipated announcement.

"I take great pleasure in announcing the engagement of Mademoiselle de Blois to the duc de Chartres!"

And we were in for yet another shock. The king returned to his council chamber, and the doors were closed behind him. Chartres, who had followed him out, looking shame-faced, now brushed by those coming forward to congratulate him and hurried across the gallery to where his mother was standing, large, square, menacing, a German pike-bearer in the full court dress of a French princess. He dropped to one knee before her and bowed his head. Without a word she dealt him a resounding box on the ear and swept from the chamber.

The tears started to my eyes. I had been critical in the past of Madame. I had even been inclined to sneer at her for her eternal letter writing to her German relatives, her passion for the hunt, her fantastic claims of Teutonic precedence in everything. She had treated me roughly on more than one occasion, accusing me of gossip and even slander. But I had to admire her now. Before the whole gallery, and knowing that she would bitterly offend the monarch whom she so deeply reverenced, she had dared to make this violent affirmation of her disapproval.

Somebody touched my hand from behind, and, turning, I found Gabrielle.

"She's the only man among us!" I exclaimed, with burning cheeks. "The rest of us deserve to be trod upon. After all, haven't we turned ourselves into carpets?"

"Ah, my dear, I know what a grief this is to you. But try to bear it with the courage you showed at Neerwinden."

"I've dished myself, and I've dished *you*," I continued bitterly. "And all for what? To see a bastard become a granddaughter of France. What a team our monarch and his brother make! The alliance of adultery and sodomy! The apotheosis of vice!"

"Please, dear, hush."

But the warning was unnecessary. Even in my wrath I had spoken in tones that would not carry. "We may as well pack our things. Our apartment will be asked for. Not later than tomorrow morning, you'll see. We'd better go to La Ferté. There's no future for us here."

"On the contrary, there's every sort of future. Now control your excitement for a minute and listen to me. While you have been working on the duc de Chartres, I have been working on his bride-to-be."

I gaped. "On Mademoiselle de Blois?"

Gabrielle nodded. "I think I can say that she and I are good friends. She is really a dear, very sincere and good, if a bit proud. She's not at all like Madame la Duchesse, whom, by the by, she rather dislikes. I have convinced her that you might be the saving of Chartres. She wants to see a lot of us after her marriage, and she has already spoken to her father, who agrees. He says you're the only friend Chartres has who is not totally dissipated. Never fear. We shall not only keep the apartment. We shall be back in favor!"

Well, I hardly knew what to say. That my wife should turn out to be so superior a courtier to myself was certainly a subject for the deepest reflection. At any rate, with a funny little drop in my spirits and a certain flatness of new outlook, I decided that I had, for the time being anyway, to accept the status quo.

"And I thought this was my last day in Versailles," I murmured.

"Whatever we accomplish, we shall accomplish *here*," Gabrielle said firmly. We were standing in the middle of the great gallery, looking down on the parterre d'eau. The fountains were playing; they were orange and tawny against the setting sun. It was time to dress for the evening reception.

Part II

1

THE CELEBRATION of the marriage between Mademoiselle de Blois and the duc de Chartres was to mark the cessation, for almost a decade and a half, of any serious effort on my part to affect the destiny of the Bourbons. I preserved all my notions of what I considered our "divine constitution." I did not alter, in the least little bit, my conception of the rule of our glorious and favored nation by a lawfully born, agnatic descendant of Hugues Capet, inspired by God and advised by his peers. But I had concluded that my role at court had better be limited to that of observer, recorder or, at the most, adviser. I should be, in other words, a historiographer rather than an actor, an eye more than a fist. It seemed to have been proved that I lacked the "happy hand."

Gabrielle, who had wanted to see me in a role, was too tactful to say that she had now changed her mind. But I felt it. I had entered the fray, and I had been worsted. Like a little boy at the seashore, I had played in the surf and been rolled by a giant wave. Gabrielle was eminently practical; she did not repine. She concentrated on our careers as courtiers; she kept her ear cocked for the news and gossip that formed the grist of my recording mill. The redeeming fact about life at Versailles was that *nothing* was too trivial to be caught and noted and lovingly preserved. Discrimination was an idle tool when one lived at the source of power. One could not have eyes and ears enough to absorb it all.

It was also true that I tended to blame myself for the emaciated condition of our scrawny second child and first son. I feared that Gabrielle's worry over my disfavor in the final days of her pregnancy might have caused this, although she never suggested such a thing herself. It seemed to me that I would do well, at least until our family was made up and succession assured, to keep myself clear of further entanglements.

There was the additional inducement, in the restoration to the royal graces of myself and my two friends, not to plunge them back in the sea of despond. Savonne had returned to court and was once again a welcome member of the circle of the mighty Maintenon, and Conti, by all reports, had the king's backing to place his bid for election to the vacant throne of Poland. So the three wretches of yesterday were now, respectively, the holder of a coveted apartment at Versailles, the intimate of the royal spouse, and a future monarch! It would be a brave man indeed who would upset *that* applecart.

And finally there was my dear mother, who gave me what my old Normandy nurse used to call the "length and breadth of her tongue." I spent an uneasy afternoon in her Paris salon, walking up and down as she made her points.

"I gather from first to last that you went against the advice of that clever little wife of yours. Oh, don't think she has betrayed you. I had it all from Savonne's mother, who had it from Madame de Maintenon herself. Things get known, as you, my dear, of all men, should know. But I hope you have learned your lesson and will be guided by Gabrielle in the future. My confidence in that girl is complete."

"But, Mother, I thought it might be taken for granted that a man should have *some* say in the direction of his life!"

"Only if he knows what he's doing."

"And who is to be the judge of that?"

"A woman! A woman who's fool enough to care for him. Her caring is what gives her the insight."

"I would never deny that Gabrielle has been the greatest help to me. Any more than I should deny that you have been. But there still have to be areas of choice reserved to men, and honor is one of these. Your sex, Mother dear, cares very little about honor. Yet you'd be the first to complain if your son let down the family standard!"

"And do you imply that interfering, officiously and unsuccessfully, with the king's plans for his own daughter and nephew is keeping up the standards of the Saint-Simons?"

"I do! Of course, you're trying to make it sound as if the king should be able to do as he wants with his own family. But his family is France, Mother! There have to be times when a man is not afraid to stand up for a principle. Even to die for one. Otherwise, there's no difference between the sexes."

Mother simply grunted at this. "I may be a foolish old woman, but I thought there were other differences. And I can't for the life of me see what you gained by opposing the king in his pet project. Didn't you know he could break you like a twig, you silly boy?"

"He can't break a principle!"

"Men can never learn to face facts. The king is a fact. Oh, you can get around him, of course. Madame de Maintenon could teach you plenty of valuable lessons in that game. But you cannot blast your way through him, and you're an idiot to try. Your father was the same way."

"My father?" I asked in amazement. "But he was always in favor. He didn't want to get around Louis XIII!"

"He was out of favor for two whole years. It was long before I knew him, before I was born, actually, but I heard it from your half-sister. It was over the fortified towns. Richelieu was intent on dismantling them. Your father thought he was going too far. He thought some of the towns in the Gironde were among the glories of France. He refused to dismantle the walls of Blaye and depended on the king's supporting him."

"And he didn't?"

"The king never went against Richelieu when Richelieu really put his foot down. That was what people never could fathom, even your father, who knew him so intimately. Louis XIII believed that Richelieu was the only man in France who could carry on the government. So, no matter how much he criticized him behind his back, when it came to a crisis, and the cardinal threatened to walk out, leaving all those mountains of paper behind, the king would simply collapse."

"And that's what happened over Blaye?"

"Yes. The towns were a vital part of Richelieu's policy. He wouldn't give in on one of them. So your father was disgraced and sent away from court. Two years later, Richelieu allowed him to come back. Your father had learned his lesson, and he remained on the best terms with the cardinal thereafter. Now our king is much more like Richelieu than like his own father. And you'd better not forget it!"

"You make me wonder if I shouldn't go with Conti to Poland!" I cried bitterly.

"That's just the kind of idiotic idea that would occur to a man. But I guess we needn't worry about it. Conti will never go."

"What makes you so sure?"

"Because, from all I hear, Madame la Duchesse will never let him!"

I had to admit that my mother was up to date. But what else did she have to do all day but give and receive gossip? I sighed and wondered what widows had talked about in the day of the Chevalier Bayard. They probably whispered that he was not really without fear or above reproach. God help us all!

2

GABRIELLE's prediction that we should again be in favor after Chartres' marriage came true, and she proposed that I take advantage of it by suggesting our names for a visit at Marly. Marly was the small but exquisite palace that the king had constructed for his weekends, and invitations there, needless to say, were passionately coveted. One proposed oneself by asking, "Sire, Marly?" as the monarch passed from his cabinet to mass. If he nodded an affirmative, one's name was placed on the list. I confess that I was very nervous, anticipating the blank stare that conveyed the royal refusal, but Gabrielle's conjecture again proved correct. Not only did I receive a nod, but it was almost a gracious one!

Marly had charm and intimacy, two qualities rarely associated with the Sun King. Indeed, the court had been generally astonished when his visits there, at first infrequent, had hardened into habit. None of us had believed that a man of his iron constitution and unslakable thirst for splendor could ever need to relax in simple surroundings. But we were wrong. The king loved Marly, which was built like a small town of marble porticos with a garden for its main square, the royal residence flanked by pavilions, one for each guest couple, connected by a colonnade. The atmosphere was informal, at least in contrast to Versailles; the king would sit of an evening with Madame de Maintenon and watch people dancing or chatting or playing cards. He would even sometimes play a hand himself, though he preferred billiards, and it was possible, if one was standing near him, to address him a question, even, on rare occasions, to tell him a joke or an amusing anecdote.

Pleasantest of all was the absence — at least on the surface — of the jealousies and animosities that pervaded the court. There was a sense, among the favored few at Marly, of having reached the social peak, of there being no place higher to climb, so that one could relax and be natural, or at least pretend to be. In heaven, with the cherubim and seraphim, what could one do but join in the celestial chorus? Versailles, like the earth, was subject to the visitation of evil spirits, but at Marly we all were blessed.

Except our new bridegroom. Chartres arrived late on Saturday and sulked in a corner at the evening reception. Even Madame de Maintenon's glare could not induce him to conceal his ill temper. His young duchess, blond and beautiful, seated with her quondam governess, seemed to proclaim, with her silent hauteur, that, sulk as he might, *she* was content with her mate. And, as he had already crudely intimated to me on the first morning after the ceremony, that at least one aspect of his marriage was all right, I deduced now that some worry other than connubial was on his mind. I went over to caution him.

"I just heard the Maintenon grumbling that you look bored. She said that, no doubt, your evenings at the Palais-royal were livelier."

"You can tell her they are. Much!"

"Please, sir, lower your voice."

"Well, why the devil should I, Saint-Simon? Who here is ever going to do anything for me? My uncle will make a fourth cousin king of Poland, but can I even hope for a regiment?"

"Is it definite about Conti, then?"

Chartres looked surprised. "I thought you heard these things even before the old trot did. Yes, it's going to be announced tonight. Conti says he has a majority of the electors. It's only been a question of whether the king will let him accept. And now he's decided that he will. Savonne's going to meet me in Paris tomorrow for a real binge. Care to join us?"

"On the Sabbath? Thank you, no."

"Well, come Monday. Or even Tuesday. This one may last a week."

"I didn't go in for that sort of thing as a bachelor, and I'm certainly not going to start now. But why is Savonne so disgusted? He wanted Conti to be king."

"He does. But he wants to go with him, and the old trot won't let him!"

I turned away from him at this, noting that Conti had just risen from his seat at the card table. I came up to him as he leaned down to draw a final card. Glancing at it, he dropped it face upwards on the table. "I am desolated, sir," he murmured, as his opponent, with a bow, pushed the chips towards him. Nobody could win with more grace. It was difficult to believe that a man of such exquisite courtesy was about to be elected to the crown of a near-barbaric country.

"Is it true?" I asked as he and I turned from the table.

"Quite true."

"Sire!" I exclaimed, giving him the royal address.

He touched his lips with the tip of his finger. "Give me two more minutes of private life. The king is about to announce it. Do you know who wants to come with me? Savonne!"

I felt my pulse quicken. "Maybe he won't be the only one!"

"You mean *you* want to come? To see that I don't abrogate the rights of the dukes?"

"Do they have dukes there?"

"If they don't, we'll have to make them. Every one a Saint-Simon!"

"Ah, sire, you're laughing at me."

"Only to keep my spirits up. Poland is a long way off. Seriously, Saint-Simon, isn't it the right thing for me to do?"

"I don't know."

"What else is there for me? It's my one chance to be somebody. And think what it will mean to my poor little wife, who spends her days dancing attendance on her old mother. After all the humiliations I've caused her, to be a queen! Fit role, at last, for a princess of the House of Condé!" And then he laughed softly at his own exaltation. "Or am I sounding like a drama of Corneille?"

"Don't forget they end as tragedies."

"And don't you be so grim! Your trouble is that you can't really believe there's a world outside Versailles. Except, perhaps, at Marly."

"Don't underestimate me, sire. Haven't I said that I might go with you?"

Conti was suddenly serious as he sensed now that I was. He placed a hand on my shoulder. "Dear friend," he said gently. Then he was silent a moment. "Perhaps I may send for you later. When all is settled there. There may be . . . yes, there may be a place for you. But I shall need you here. At first, anyway. Someone, as you may conceive, is very unhappy about all this."

"She doesn't show it." We both glanced to where Madame la Duchesse was making herself the animated center of the group around Madame de Maintenon.

"Did you think she would?" His hand gripped my shoulder tightly. "Stay, my friend, and keep an eye on her. Poland is not for you."

"We'll see about that!"

There was a rustle of rising as the king now walked to the center of the room. He waved an arm towards Conti.

"Ladies and gentlemen, I present to you the king of Poland!"

A burst of applause followed, and the king, nodding graciously to Conti, immediately left the room, followed by Madame de Maintenon. Conti was at once surrounded by a circle of congratulating friends, and I moved over to observe Madame la Duchesse.

Everybody near her, of course, was discussing Conti, and the remarks, particularly of the ladies, were maliciously designed to try her endurance. It was cruel, but how many chances did courtiers have to "get back" at a king's daughter? She was frequently hard enough on them! Here is a sample of their comments:

"What a happy day for Conti! He must be quite overjoyed."

"Isn't it splendid, dear Madame, that we should have the House of Bourbon represented on *two* thrones?"

"Do you think the new king will have many regrets at leaving poor old Versailles?"

"Surely not! With such a glorious future he will forget us all in a week's time!"

"What will he call himself? François premier? Of course! As gallant as his namesake."

Madame la Duchesse suddenly threw back her head and laughed with a gaiety it was hard to believe was feigned.

"I don't suppose there are many of us here who would be difficult to forget!" she exclaimed. "No, if I were going to Warsaw, I should have no need of amnesia. The only thing I do not envy my fortunate cousin is the loss of his sovereign. How can it be a happy event to leave the court of the king you all profess to adore?"

When the princesse de Conti, tiny, dark and dour, approached the circle, Madame la Duchesse rose and curtsied low to the new queen. The latter's eyes glittered.

"You must pity us, dear cousin," she said with a simpering smile. "We leave you in God's country while we travel north to the land of ice and snow! How shall we manage without your wit and warmth?"

"Ah, my dear, you will be in Poland what you have been here: the winter queen!"

It was typical of her wit. Everyone knew that her term referred to the sexual temperature of Conti's wife.

But I was now in for a surprise. As Madame la Duchesse left the group and passed me, she rapped me lightly on the knuckles with her fan and indicated with a brief but imperious nod that I was to follow her. In the gallery, she seated herself on a divan and pointed to the chair beside it.

"I have a bone to pick with you, Monsieur de Saint-Simon. You were sitting there as if you were at a comedy. As if I were putting it all on!"

"If it was a performance, it was a splendid one! If not, it was a touching tribute to a great prince. Either way, I applaud."

"Why should I not be glad to see the prince de Conti king of Poland? Do you think it is pleasant for me to see a man of his ability wasting his time at court? Do you think I care nothing for his advancement? For his glory?"

"I think you will miss him. As will we all."

"Of course, I shall miss him! I shall miss him horribly. You know all about that. You're his friend. But you think I care only for my own satisfaction. It never occurs to you that I could put his best interests ahead of myself!"

I looked at those dark flashing eyes and marveled at her candor. "You honor me with your confidence, Madame."

"And you wonder why? I'll tell you. It's because you hold Conti in your heart."

I hesitated. "He does me the honor to call me his friend."

"Friend? I know nothing about friendship. I know about love. You and I *love* Conti."

I stared at the duchess in alarm and fascination. What on earth did she mean? And how did she know about my emotions? I had told Conti, of course, about my devotion to my father and to the duc de Beauvillier. Perhaps he had told her about my cult of loyalty. But how could she equate this with her passion for Conti? And yet — somehow — as I looked into those mocking, smiling eyes, I seemed to sense a depth behind them.

"How do you mean . . ." I stammered, "when you say that I . . . love the prince?"

"Oh, I don't mean like his pages, if that's what worries you," she replied with a snort. "I don't accuse you of that."

"Surely, ma'am, you don't believe such gossip!" I exclaimed, scandalized at the casual way in which she threw this off.

"Never mind what I believe. What have such matters to do with me? I've spent my life at court, and if I've learned anything, it's not to let the few good things that happen to me be spoiled by the bad. Conti and I, that's a box, a precious one, and I keep it tightly closed, except when I open the lid just a crack, like this, when I'm talking to you; and that's only because he said I could trust you! But you don't think I pop my husband into that box, or his wife, or my children, or his? Or anyone or anything else? Never! I'm not such an ass."

"Why do you tell me all this?" I asked, bewildered.

"Because when he goes to Poland, you and he will write each other, and I will give you messages. Oh, don't look at me that way! I shan't shock you. You won't have to put in anything you don't choose. And he will do the same, in his letters to you. There! Does that disgrace you? Does that make you a bawd? Think of it, my dear duke; I may never see him again!"

Her eyes sparkled, but not with tears, and I took her hand and raised it gravely to my lips.

"If he becomes a great king," I murmured fervently, "I know where he will have learned his trade."

"It's a scene from Corneille, isn't it?" she replied, but then she spoiled it all with that terrible mocking laugh. I felt like a fool.

"I may not, after all, be available for your correspondence," I observed dryly.

"Ah, traitor, why?"

"Because I may wish to share his glory!"

"You mean you want to go with him?" Madame la Duchesse, raising her eyebrows starkly, actually looked like her father. "Not till we tell you, anyway. We need you *here*."

3

THE PRINCE DE CONTI departed for Poland, with Savonne on his staff, for Madame de Maintenon finally let him go. For some weeks we had no news, but after they were established in Warsaw I heard regularly from both. The news was not good. The elector of Saxony had entered the contest for the throne and had gathered considerable support from the nobles in the north. There seemed a distinct possibility of civil war. My information was slower than the official couriers because my correspondents had to wait until a messenger whom they trusted was going to France. We could not take the risk of being opened by the king's police spies.

Conti's letters to me, which I turned over to Madame la Duchesse, were eloquent. He seemed thoroughly absorbed in the business of winning adherents, and supplied me with all kinds of interesting details about politics in that murky, northern world, but each letter invariably ended with a nostalgic evocation of what he had left behind at Versailles.

"Perhaps it is just as well that things ended when they did. I wonder how much longer the envious court would have allowed us to go on as we were going. People resent what is unique. They could see that between her and myself there was something that never could have been engendered between either of us and any other person, something that seemed to have no real relation to either of us taken alone."

It was perfectly true. There was a glow between Conti and Madame la Duchesse that had seemed at times to awe even their angry and jealous spouses, that had almost silenced the objections even of Madame de Maintenon and the king. Simply to see them together in the garden at Marly, or sitting beside each other at the comedy, smiling and chatting like the most proper in-laws, was to receive the impression of a bond that was all the stronger for having been adapted to the public gaze. Although they were both intensely physical and passionate beings, they seemed to communicate on a level above or beyond the senses. Perhaps that was simply because they made the rest of us feel a bit quaint, a bit ridiculous, even, at times, irrelevant. The most striking thing about their passion was that it appeared to dignify them. Madame la Duchesse seemed less trival, less malicious, certainly less heartless, when she was with Conti, whereas he with her seemed stronger, more resolute, less inclined to see the world as a decaying and purposeless planet.

"What keeps me going is the sense that I have been granted the greatest boon a man can have in her love, and now the Almighty, or providence, or simply the community of man, is requiring that I give something back to the world in return. If I ever establish my crown, there will be no end of things that I can accomplish here. Think of it, Saint-Simon! A prince of the blood who may actually be of service to his fellow men!"

Madame la Duchesse became very intimate with Gabrielle and myself in these days. She professed to follow the Polish proceedings with the deepest interest and never showed by so much as a blink of the eye that she was afflicted by the prospect of her lover's permanent displacement. On the contrary, she seemed full of hopes for his glory and would say that we should all be known in the pages of history as mere footnotes to his great career!

"Of course, *you* may be something more, Monsieur de Saint-Simon," she told me one afternoon when Gabrielle and I had met her, as appointed, by Neptune's Basin. "You may be his first minister."

"What makes you say that, ma'am?" Gabrielle asked. "How could the king of Poland have a subject of our king as his first minister?"

"Well, as long as your husband was willing to live in Warsaw, his nationality would make no difference."

"And *is* my husband willing to live in Warsaw?" Gabrielle faced me with a look of calm inquiry.

"It's an idea I've played with," I admitted, in some embarrassment. I had not wished to upset Gabrielle before any final decisions were taken.

"Would it not be good of you to inform me, before transporting your wife and infants to a land of snow and ice?"

Madame la Duchesse glanced, I thought rather maliciously, from me to my wife. It always pleased her to uncover family dissension.

"You would be given plenty of time, my dear," I assured Gabrielle as blandly as I could, "before anything so drastic was asked of you. Who knows? If I did go, it might be only for a few months at a time, on an advisory basis."

"And I should be left alone here, at Versailles?"

It was the first time that Gabrielle had ever crossed me — at least in the presence of a great person. I was surprised.

"You would always be at liberty to come with me."

"There!" cried Madame la Duchesse. "Can you want more than that, my dear? *I* couldn't. Why, I should love to go to Poland this very minute!"

"With small children, ma'am?"

"The smaller the better! They wouldn't get in my way when I was there."

The only way that one could perceive the strain on Madame la Duchesse was in her increased acerbity with members of the royal family. Her younger sister, the new duchesse de Chartres, who now, as a granddaughter-in-law of France, outranked the wife of a prince of the blood, particularly irked her. In marriage contracts witnessed by the king and his children, where Madame la Duchesse now had to sign under her sister, she would style herself "Louise-Françoise de Bourbon — *legitimated*" in large handwriting to call attention to the fact that Madame de Chartres always omitted the humiliating qualification. And at a performance of *Esther* she actually hissed the reference to the disgrace of the "haughty Vashti," notoriously inserted by Racine as a compliment to Madame de Maintenon at the expense of Madame la Duchesse's mother. Yet when she was seen the next day emerging from her "stepmother's" apartment after what was assumed to have been one of the Maintenon's famous dressings down, her eyes were not red, as in the case of other scolded princesses, but clear and defiant.

Matters were not going well in Poland. It began to look as if the whole project might fail. Conti now found that he had problems with French as well as Polish support. One evening at home I read Gabrielle this part of one of his letters:

"The king expects me to back French policy in everything, particularly in Spain. On the death of King Charles, which can't be far off now, he and the emperor will both claim the throne by descent. Charles is supposed to be supporting the French claim in his will, and it is generally believed that our king would pass the Spanish crown on to one of his grandsons. I feel very strongly that it would be disastrous to have Versailles and Madrid that closely linked. It might unite all Europe against France in a terrible war."

Gabrielle made no comment. She simply reached out her hand for the letter. I did not give it to her.

"I think this one is *not* for the eyes of Madame la Duchesse."

"I thought they all were. I thought that was the understanding."

"Ah, but you forget my discretion. Madame la Duchesse is a very loose talker. If the king got wind of the views of his Polish candidate towards his great goal — Spain — all would be over."

"You mean the prince de Conti would be recalled?"

"And his kingdom would disappear like a dream! We can hardly put a weapon like that in the hands of a woman who wants him home."

Gabrielle looked at me curiously. "I thought you thought she was so noble. So disinterested. Like a heroine of Corneille's. You did rather go on about it, dear!"

"Well, why tempt people? If Madame la Duchesse asks you, say that we have not heard from Conti this week."

Gabrielle nodded obediently. "Just so. The posts are terrible!"

As it turned out, that was the last letter I had from Conti. Some weeks later a majority of the Polish nobles went over to the elector of Saxony, and the game was up. There was nothing for my poor hero to do but creep ignominiously back to Versailles.

4

*T*HE APARTMENTS of the duc and duchesse de Bourbon in the great south wing were very splendid. Monsieur le Duc had hung the walls, as if he had been at his own château at Chantilly, with the same vast, bloody battle scenes that his grandfather, the Great Condé, had used to show Conti as a boy. Of course, in so trying to deflect attention from his own minimal war career, he drew attention rather violently to it. Interspersed with these pictures of carnage were big, pompous Rigaud portraits of Condé warriors in brilliant armor, with further slaughter going on in the background.

Monsieur le Duc was a tiny man, like all the Condés. His father, the great hero's son, had cared more for genealogical than physical splendor and, by marrying a Palatine princess, had blighted his posterity with the dwarfishness of the Gonzagas. The slight stature of Monsieur le Duc was not improved, either, by a pot belly, but, although one of the most malicious men in court, he could be very bright and witty, and I always enjoyed an occasional chat with him on a neutral subject.

The first time that I saw the prince de Conti after his return from Poland was at a small reception in the apartments of the duc and duchesse de Bourbon. Madame la Duchesse was at her most exuberant. She made no secret of her delight at being reunited with her adored one, and she strolled with him among her other guests, arm in arm. Monsieur le Duc, who could hardly make open objection to such cordiality to a returning brother-in-law, was nonetheless obviously irritated. When he and I talked, he allowed his tone to be grating.

"A sad day for France, sir," I observed discreetly.

"For France," he emphasized. "Not, necessarily, for all Frenchmen. Or all French women."

"I suppose it is only natural for the royal family to rejoice at the return of so beloved a member."

"Rather too natural, Monsieur de Saint-Simon."

"Poland has lost a great sovereign. And we, a great ally. I suppose there can be no doubt about that?"

"Can there not?"

"You doubt the capacity of the prince de Conti?"

"I doubt his enthusiasm."

"You mean you believe he had no heart for the job?"

"I mean he had not the slightest intention of ever becoming king of Poland. It was the title he wanted, pure and simple. He calculated that if elected and then deposed, he could return to Versailles and take precedence over the rest of the family (including your humble servant), the way the deposed king of England does."

"But surely it was understood from the beginning that an elective crown would be recognized only if the election held!"

"Was it?" Monsieur le Duc's eyebrows soared. "Not by Conti, it wasn't. He believed that my wife would intercede with the king. And it is entirely possible that she may have. But the king was not going to flout the wishes of the first prince of the blood." Here he made me a jaunty little mocking bow. "Not even at the request of the first princess!"

"It seems difficult to believe," I continued, placing no credit whatever in what my jealous interlocutor had said, "that we could have all been saying our prayers for the fruition of a project that its principal beneficiary wished to abort."

"*All* the prayers were not directed to that goal. There may even have been masses offered for the *failure* of the project. Black masses!"

This was going rather far. The duchess's mother, Madame de Montespan, was notoriously supposed to have sought to preserve the king's love by a black mass, in which blood from the slit throat of a newborn infant had been allowed to drip on her stomach as she lay, naked and supine, on an improvised altar.

I decided to leave Monsieur le Duc to his morbid reflections, and, bowing, turned to make my way towards his wife. Seeing me, she waved and pulled Conti to the middle of the chamber, where we met.

"Oh, don't make such a face," she reproached me. "I have to have my little moment. I am quite aware that it infuriates Monsieur le Duc. But I'll make it up to him. I always do. If you don't permit yourself some little outlets in court life, you'll find yourself exploding in little pieces all over the great gallery."

"I am very happy to see you, sir," I said to Conti.

"Saint-Simon, dear fellow!" He detached himself from Madame la Duchesse to embrace me warmly. She burst out laughing.

"Well! Perhaps I should leave you two boys alone!"

"Perhaps it would be good if you did," Conti advised her gently. "For a minute, anyway. You've made enough of me. Go and un-ruffle Monsieur le Duc. He looks like a startled grouse." Alone, he turned to me. "I can never thank you enough for your letters. What are people saying? That I made a lovely mess of it?"

"No," I replied judiciously. "Most consider it simply bad luck. Some blame the king. A few, like Monsieur le Duc, think you didn't really try. That you wanted all the time to come home. For what reason, you can imagine."

"I give you my solemn word, Saint-Simon, that I tried my best!" He was graver than I had ever seen him, very pale but with a flash in his eyes. "I did everything a man could do to win over the nobles to my candidacy. But when I saw that it was all to no avail, that I was to be flung out of that cold, dark northern heaven back to the glittering lights of old Versailles, when I saw that my allies were dissolving . . . well, despise me if you will . . . I was actually happy. Oh, happy as I had never been! To come back, a broken Antony, to my serpent of old Nile! For that's what she is, my friend. I'm in her clutches now forever."

"There are other careers," I insisted, shocked.

"Not for me. How you stare, Saint-Simon! Do you think I don't know myself? I had a chance, one single glorious chance, a golden opportunity, and it's gone. There are people who never get second chances, and I am one of them. I can even stand back and admire my own futility. My story is short but elegantly written. Charming, if a bit sad. Never tragic. I was wrong, just now, to compare myself to Antony. I am more like a perfect little novel by Madame de La Fayette."

I could not avoid the feeling that there was a constraint in Conti's manner. It was not only the note of self-dramatization in his voice. I had a distinct impression that he was putting up a wall of words between himself and me, not only that I might be prevented from criticizing him, but that he might be kept from criticizing *me*. Yet, what had I done that was wrong, except perhaps encourage him in the illusion that his love could be maintained by correspondence when a clean break should have been advocated? What lover would have held *that* against a friend?

Others pushed forward now to speak to Conti, and I had to give way. I thought that he would send for me in private, but he did not do so. And something else troubled me at this time. Savonne had not only failed to return to court; he had not even written to me.

One of Conti's staff had told me that Savonne had been gravely depressed by the failure of the enterprise and had spoken of making a religious retreat. This was not unlike him, but his silence was. As none of his family was at court, I was constrained to write a note to one of Madame de Maintenon's secretaries to ask if they had news of him. What was my astonishment to be informed in return that the great marquise would see me herself! I was instructed to present myself at her apartments the very next morning, before she departed on her daily visit to St.-Cyr.

5

*A*T THE APPOINTED TIME I was shown into Madame de
Maintenon's receiving room, where she was seated in the
famous red chair. I was not invited to be seated.

"I decided that it would be better if I spoke to you directly,
Monsieur de Saint-Simon," she began in a chilling tone. "My
cousin Savonne has not been willing to communicate with you. I
am afraid he no longer regards you as his friend."

"May I ask the reason?" I inquired, in great agitation.

"He has been bitterly upset over this Polish business. Almost, I
fear, to the risk of his sanity."

"That is understandable. But why should it make him cease to
regard me as his friend?"

The Maintenon honored me with an impassive stare. "You have
not been one of *my* friends, sir."

"What causes Madame to think that?"

"In court these things are known."

"In court, I suppose, we are at the mercy of every gossip. But I
hardly supposed that the lady who has been described by the king
himself as a priestess of the life of reason would listen to idle
tattle."

"I listen to everything! I have to. Look at the crowd waiting outside this room, just for a word with me, before I go to Saint-Cyr.
Every last one of them has a favor to ask or a tale to tell. Usually
both!"

I allowed myself to give her a narrow look. "You may find many who will misquote me. You will not find one who can have misread me."

"What on earth do you mean by that?"

"Simply that I have never had the presumption to name Madame de Maintenon in a letter."

"And why should I be concerned with your letters, sir?" She paused here, and then, to my astonishment, smiled. "Oh, of course, you think I read everyone's mail."

"Letters *have* been read, Madame."

"I don't know what measures may be taken by the ministers in the interests of security. But contrary to popular opinion *I* read only letters that are addressed to me." I bowed in silence. Contradiction was hardly expected. "Of course, people suspect me. My position invites that. But I do the job God gave me as best I can." She did not raise her eyes to the ceiling as she said this; she was too clever for that. She simply allowed her eyelids to droop for a moment. "A very poor best, I'm sure it is."

"No one doubts your devotion to duty, Madame."

"Oh, do they not? Do *you* not, sir? When one is reared as I was, on a lonely island, thousands of leagues away, across the ocean, and then is doomed to live in a crowded court, one has experienced the extremes of isolation and inundation. Thank heaven I learned to depend on myself before I was subjected to the scrutinies of Versailles. But I didn't ask you here to recriminate. Or even to win you to my side. No, I shall be quite candid. I asked you here to tell you something that it is in your best interests for you to know."

Again I bowed and waited.

"You are aware, sir, of my great interest in the king's children. When I was honored, many years ago, with the charge of the royal infants, I accepted it as a duty. I did not know then that it would become a joy. I have learned to love them as I might have loved my own. Not least in my affection is Madame la Duchesse."

"She is indeed a radiant princess."

"Thank you. I believe she is. But I do not imagine that I am revealing any startling news when I say that she is indiscreet. I believed that it would be a good thing for everybody if the prince de Conti were elected king of Poland. I believed that you, too, saw matters in that light."

"It is an honor to be of your persuasion, Madame."

Madame de Maintenon did not concede by so much as a blink that she understood my irony. "The king, sir, is always a monarch first and a father second. He would never consider a possible advantage to a daughter if the smallest French interest were at stake. So the moment he suspected that the prince de Conti might not share his views as to the Spanish succession, the prince's candidacy was dead."

I waited, but she did not continue. "And *did* the king have such suspicions?" I demanded at last.

"How could he not, when Madame la Duchesse told him so herself? It annoyed him that she should be the one to bring about what she so evidently and inappropriately desired, namely, the recall of the prince, but that could not affect his decision."

I stared. "And I am to conclude that you believe me somehow to have had a hand in this?"

"Don't play games with *me,* sir. You showed Madame la Duchesse the prince's letter!"

My mind stumbled. All became dark about me. *"I* did! And why should I have done that?"

"Wasn't it your agreement? You're not the only man who has been a willing tool of Madame la Duchesse. My poor cousin Savonne was heartbroken when he learned of your treachery." She raised her hand sternly as I stepped forward in shock. "It was *his* term, sir, not mine. And I very much doubt if he will wish to see you again. He may even decide to take holy orders. I shall have to be sure, of course, that he has a proper vocation and is not taking so drastic a step in the heat of temporary emotion."

"Madame, I beg you to listen to me. I . . ."

"That will be all, Monsieur de Saint-Simon. You have interfered in a matter that concerned a member of the royal family who is very dear to me. I simply wanted you to know that I *knew*."

* * *

Half-distracted, I wandered in a daze through the corridors of the palace, failing to acknowledge nods or bows. Gabrielle was crossing the great gallery with two ladies. The moment she saw me she must have sensed that something was wrong, for she left her friends and hurried across the floor to me.

"What's wrong? You have the most ghastly pallor! Are you ill?"

I looked at her in horror. "You betrayed me! You betrayed me to Madame la Duchesse!"

She glanced quickly to her left and right. "Let us go home," she whispered.

"No! Here! I must talk to you here!"

Gabrielle was quick to accept situations and make the best of them. She walked at once to the emptiest portion of the gallery and turned to face me, her back against one of those immense silver *guéridons* supporting two tall silver candelabra, which framed her patiently resolute countenance. I remember that the stems of the candelabra were wrought in the forms of naked wrestling men. Gabrielle struck me, even at such a moment, as affecting a pose of female superiority to such idle muscular strife.

"You gave Conti's letter about Spain to Madame la Duchesse!"

Gabrielle's unaltered expression disclosed to me now that she had been prepared for my outburst. Despite her calm, I suspected that her heart must have been beating faster than usual.

"Was that not your agreement with her?" she asked.

"What do you mean?"

"That you would show her everything the prince had written?"

"Only what he had written about herself. And then only at my discretion. Good God, do you know what you've *done?*"

"Perfectly. I've done exactly what the prince wanted."

"Woman, you're mad!"

"Be calm, my dear, I beg of you. The prince was desperate to find a way to come home. Why else would he blab his intention to controvert the king in his most cherished scheme? One whiff of that at Versailles, and the Polish venture was done for! Oh, don't you *see* it?" Gabrielle's eyes were desperately earnest now; she had even clasped her hands. "And he *is* home, without disgrace — for there was no treason in a Polish king not wanting a Bourbon on the Spanish throne — and reunited with his adored duchess. If you weren't so blinded by your ideas of Conti's greatness, you'd admit I'd done a good day's work. Anyone can see he'd have made the most ghastly sovereign!"

I was beside myself. "Don't give me such rot! You just didn't want to go to Poland yourself! Admit it!"

Gabrielle looked down at the floor. It came across to me suddenly that she was not in the least afraid — nervous, but not afraid. "Ah, now, you want my real motive. Very well, you shall have it." She looked up and fixed her eyes with sudden sternness on mine. "I would have been glad to go to Poland. I would have been glad to go to the ends of the earth with you — if it would have made you happy. But there's only one place in the world where you can be happy, and that's right here. At court."

"It's the only place in the world where I'm utterly miserable!"

"It's where you're alive, anyway. You accuse me of reading your letters. I plead guilty! And not only your letters. I've read all your notes, your memoranda, even your journal! I've read every scrap of paper in our whole house. And I know what you are at last. What you really are. You're not really a duke or a soldier or even a courtier. You're a writer!"

What was most extraordinary about this revelation was that I had no clear idea of whether or not Gabrielle thought this was an honorable thing to be. I somehow received the impression that what she was trying to say was that it was her duty to find out what was my real profession and then to support me in it. But there it was again, the idea that Gabrielle perhaps shared with my mother: that whatever a man *did* decide to be would probably be a bit ridiculous. And I could now see by the glint in her eyes that she fully expected to be forgiven for what she had done. Perhaps even applauded!

"Gabrielle!" I cried in exasperation. "Do you realize you may have destroyed a man's career? That you may have twisted history?"

"Oh, don't you think things come out pretty much the same, no matter what one does? I never really believed the prince was going to be elected, did you?"

"Of course I did!"

"Well, what does it matter who's king of Poland?"

"Gabrielle . . ." I stopped, too outraged, too flabbergasted, to go on. I might as well have been talking to the candlesticks. It was so evident that she, like my mother, would never, never believe that reality and normality, and probably even utopia, were not what she had before her very eyes in Versailles, on that day, under the great king, living in the great century. Of course, she did not believe in God! She believed only in the here, the now. And then my anger, even part of my sorrow, seemed to ebb away into the swelling, bubbling stream of the evident futility of it all. "At least you can write to Savonne and tell him whose fault it was," I growled. "The poor man thinks I betrayed him."

"Oh, I'll be happy to do that!" Gabrielle replied briskly, delighted to find so practical a way out of what threatened to be a hopeless impasse. "In fact, I'll go and do it this **very minute!**"

And she left me staring into my silly countenance in the great, smoky, silver-framed mirror behind her.

6

———————◆———————

A s I stated at the commencement of this exercise, my purpose
is to give some explanation, or at least some account, of how
I came to write my memoirs. So I am deliberately selecting the
events, or episodes, of my life that have most bearing on that, which
means that I shall shortly have occasion to skip over some dozen
years. It was not, I cannot too much emphasize, that these skipped
passages of time were unhappy or even unfruitful; it is simply
that they were not relevant, at least in my opinion, to the chosen
topic.

At the time of the failure of Conti's Polish aspirations, I had resolved to eschew the life of political action for that of a historiographer, and I remained more or less faithful to this resolution from
1697 to 1709, the year of the marriage of the king's third legitimate
grandson, the duc de Berry, to which I shall advert in a near chap-
ter. During all these dozen or more years I stayed at court, noting
everything, recording everything, and trying my hand at essays and
tracts on various subjects, such as the story of certain ducal houses
or the rights of peers in the parlements. I had not decided what
form my ultimate work would take, but I had an idea that it
would be extensive: a history of the peerage, or a history of our
kings, or maybe even a history of France itself. But whatever the
end result, everything at court was happily relevant to it, either
in the light that it shed on the past or in the light that it shed on
the present. My research was without limits and without waste.

I always like to tie up loose ends; I was never a dangler; so I shall fill in here the unhappy balance of my poor friend Conti's short life, which lasted until the year of Berry's marriage, when (quite coincidentally) I again turned my thoughts to political action. But before I do this, let me trace something of my own and Gabrielle's domestic development in those same years.

It took me a long time to accept what I sometimes regarded as her perfidy, and sometimes as her simple perversity, in the matter of Conti's letter. She always insisted that she had merely carried out my own declared policy of transmitting all of his correspondence to Madame la Duchesse, and that, as a trustworthy agent, she should have been given the discretion to ignore the single, improper exception that I had quixotically insisted upon. When I pointed out that she at the time had supplied a different motive, namely, her wish to keep me from going to Poland, she would shrug and repeat that we were duty bound by our agreement with the lovers to relay *all* the correspondence. Obviously, she had decided, after due reflection, that this was the best possible face to put on her betrayal of my confidence, and with this decision made, womanlike, she made it the truth for herself. I had either to accept it or to face the misery of a domestic life where my wife was no longer my ally.

I accepted it. I had reached the point where I could no longer endure the prospect of court life without a confidant, a supporter, a sharer of pangs and joys. Savonne was not deep enough to understand me; Conti and Chartres were too much above me in rank; Beauvillier was too old. I had no end of friendly acquaintances, and, because I knew how to listen well, I was the repository of the secrets of half the court, but all that was not the same as intimacy. I had never had intimates, perhaps because I could never tell my own secrets to anyone but myself — or to Gabrielle. Yes, I had told Gabrielle everything because I had taken for granted, with the seeming docility of her acceptance of my masterhood, that she was another version of myself. I suppose many men have made that same mistake and then have awakened to find that the keys of the fortress have been surrendered, not to the enemy surely, but to another occupant of the citadel, and that the siege of oneself, which is what life is all about, is being defended by a new captain, whose strategy seems only sometimes well taken.

The most I could hope for in our new settlement was an equal partnership. Gabrielle was always perfectly respectful to me in her outward demeanor, both in company and in private — she avoided the vulgarity of adjusting herself to the public stare — but she had given up being silent when she disagreed with me on points of any importance. She would never interrupt, and she was never, thank goodness, shrill; she would not even raise her voice. She would simply wait until there was a proper pause, and then she would state, just once and with perfect clarity, her view. Oh, yes, considering the viragos one had seen at court, I had much to be thankful for!

My mother once pointed out to me that at court the sexes were equal. There were no battles to be fought there, no bread to be won, and the emphasis on clothes and etiquette certainly offered no particular advantage to males. My tools were my eyes and ears, and Gabrielle's were every bit as acute as mine. If I alone had access to the levers and couchers of the king, she could penetrate to areas where I could not follow: the boudoirs of Madame de Maintenon and the duchesse de Bourgogne. It only made sense that we should operate as a team. Of course, it was painful to me to suspect that many of my values Gabrielle did not share. She was much more inclined than I, for example, to accept the authority of the king in matters of precedence, and she was certainly more tolerant of the low state of morals at court. She proclaimed herself, in short, a realist. But there was no basic reason, I supposed, that a realist and an idealist should not work together.

A good home is based on compromise, and I compromised. I gave up trying to conform Gabrielle's views to my own. I listened carefully to her advice, without always taking it. In return, she accepted my decisions. She never nagged, never recriminated, and, best of all, never said "I told you so." And about our three children, our unhappily undersized sons (now two) and daughter, we never had the smallest disagreement. There were times when I suspected that this was the result of a certain maternal indifference on Gabrielle's part, but she performed all her outward duties to her offspring with the greatest propriety. As for myself, did she love me or did she own me? Perhaps a little of each. She never, at any rate, gave the least indication of not being content with her lot. There have surely been millions of worse marriages.

The terrible war that Conti had predicted over the Spanish succession broke out at last in 1702, with England, Holland and the German empire arrayed against us to determine whether or not the dauphin's second son, the duc d'Anjou, should reign in Madrid as Philippe V. Conti himself managed to serve briefly in the campaign in northern Italy, but he was recalled at the instigation of his jealous fellow general, the duc de Vendôme, another royal bastard, or at least the descendant of one, being a great-grandson of Henri IV and Gabrielle d'Estrée. It was Conti's doom, like that of our fair land, to be brought low by the illicit spawn of royalty. One wondered if there would ever be an end to it. He idled his remaining years away at court, drinking more, dissipating more, doing more of everything than he should have done, until his death at forty-five in 1709, just before the hectic business about the duc de Berry's marriage.

I shall not linger unduly over the sad story of my poor friend's decomposition. I saw him less frequently in these years, as it became evident that there was little or nothing that I could do for him. At first I used to lecture him. I would spend whole mornings in his apartment, warning him of the folly of his course, begging him to apply to the king for any post abroad, even an embassy, although such was beneath his rank, but it was all to no avail.

"Give it up, Saint-Simon," he would say with his sad smile and melancholy eyes. "Give it up, and give me up. I'm not worth it. I'm through. Don't you think a man of my intelligence knows when he's through?"

"No!"

But much good my vehemence did me. I appealed to everyone. I appealed even to Madame la Duchesse. I was mad enough to think that she might allow him to leave her again, and I was bold enough to strike the note that only with the challenge of some post away from court would he be able to preserve what was left of his manhood.

"There is enough of it left for me, Monsieur de Saint-Simon," she replied, with snapping eyes. "Even if there is not enough for *you.*"

But, alas, she begged the very question I was putting. For Madame la Duchesse was a fascinating and at times horrible combination of a beautiful woman and a praying mantis. She was perfectly, almost sublimely, capable of every contradiction. She wanted her lover here at Versailles, quite at her disposal, and at the same time with the reputation of a warrior and hero. She would share him with wine bottles and page boys, the temptations of idleness, but not with soldiers at the front. There were moments when I felt that she almost welcomed his degradation as ensuring her own possession, and other times when she may have fancied that he was eluding her, oozing out between the grasp of her fingers through the liquid properties of his vices. Perhaps she simply wanted to destroy him in order that no one else should have him.

Certainly the worst thing that she did to him was her affair with her sister's husband, my old friend Chartres, or Orléans, as he was styled after the death of Monsieur. Of course, part of her motivation in this may have been to score a point over a younger sister who had had the good fortune to marry a higher-ranking prince, but I believe an equally strong one was her perverse desire to torture Conti for letting himself become less of a man than Orléans.

For the reluctant bridegroom of Mademoiselle de Blois ("Madame Lucifer," as we called her because of her insufferable pride) was, for all his failings, very much a man. Sometimes I thought of him as the only man in the whole court. Except, perhaps, the king, who, incidentally, was the only man of whom Orléans was afraid, despite all his surly bluff and apparent defiance.

When I protested to Orléans that he was not only undoing himself fatally with the king by sleeping with two of his daughters at once, but cruelly wounding our old friend Conti, he took up my first point first, answering me in his usual crude, blunt manner.

"I thought you'd congratulate me, Saint-Simon! We've lost the war against the bastards in the salon; let us win it in the bed-chambers. My uncle has married all his bastards into the royal family; he wants to have them screwed by Bourbons in wedlock. Well, I'm arranging to have them screwed by a Bourbon out of wedlock! I've even put the dowager Conti on my list, but she's a tough piece of meat to handle."

I should explain here that Conti's deceased older brother had married the king's oldest bastard by the Vallière. The dowager princesse de Conti, although in my opinion still a fine-looking woman, was some years older than Orléans and myself.

"I don't see how you can give a good account of yourself to a woman you dislike," I observed, with a grimace.

"I don't dislike Madame la Duchesse," he retorted with a growl. "She's a damn fine creature. I disapprove of her, that's all."

"You mean that the 'damn fine creature' happens to be a . . . ?" I paused to raise my eyebrows.

"A bitch. Exactly." Orléans was not one to leave an *i* undotted. "It can be great fun to have an affair with a bitch. You ought to try it some day, Saint-Simon. It might take your mind off the all-absorbing question of whether you shouldn't be the thirteenth instead of the fourteenth ranking duke of the realm."

"What does Madame Lucifer say to all this?" I demanded, ignoring his last observation.

"Well, it's very odd, but I think she prefers to have me confine my infidelities to the royal family. You know what they say about my wife, don't you? That she's a princess, even on . . ." He waited, smiling, for me to finish.

"Even on her closed stool? You *do* hear everything."

"Well, I pick up the smut while you pick up the gossip. But, seriously, to come back to our friend Conti, I thought it might do him good to see his lovely duchess as she is. For don't think I've been her only diversion. Far from it! I even figured that the king might send me back to the Spanish front to get rid of me. And maybe I could persuade Conti to go along. It might be the saving of him."

I stared, astonished to find such evidence of good will under the appearance of betrayal. But that was Orléans' way.

"I'm afraid it's a bit late for that now. Conti's not well enough for a campaign."

"Nonsense. A little less wine, a little more exercise, and we'll bring him around."

But there was no basis, alas, for such optimism. My poor old friend and hero was dying. Of what he was dying I did not know, but his skin was, if possible, even paler, and his eyes, dry now, had a funny fixed little glitter. He spent less time at court and more in his house in Paris. The last time I visited him there he was stretched out on a divan, clad in a long blue robe. He simply gazed out the window while I told him the news from Versailles, but when I had finished, he said something that I shall always remember.

"You must write down these things, Saint-Simon. You have a style of your own. Or perhaps I should say, a style of your era. It's odd, but very few people in any era have its style. Most people might belong to almost any era as well as their own. And there are some who belong to only one, and it's often their misfortune not to live in it. I, for example, should have lived in the Rome of Marcus Aurelius. Madame la Duchesse should have been a great courtesan in Byzantium. And Orléans . . . I don't know. I suspect that his era may not yet have come. But if a man has a contemporary style, he should certainly express it. In words or pictures or music or buildings. That is how we hang history, on pegs. Otherwise it would be a hopeless jumble. You *are* Louis XIV. You and the king. Perhaps there are only two of you, after all."

He smiled his charming smile when I rose to take my leave, and stretched out his poor thin hand.

"Goodbye, Saint-Simon. Man of our time."

There were tears in my eyes. "I'll come back, sir. Soon."

"You will find me gone. But do not be sad for me. I shall be quite happy in the court of the Antonines!"

Three days later he was dead. The king ordered a week of court mourning. Madame la Duchesse betrayed by not so much as a quiver or a blink the extent of her desolation. It must have helped her to know that a thousand eyes were trying to ferret out her secret.

Part III

1

BY 1709 the War of the Spanish Succession had been fought on three fronts for eight years, and we had lost much of the territory that we had gained in the earlier, more successful conflicts of the reign. Worse still was the prospect of the invasion of our land by British, Dutch and German troops under Marlborough and Prince Eugène. In Spain, Philippe V still clung to the throne on which his grandfather had precariously placed him, but half his country was in enemy hands. Louis XIV had now been king for sixty-six years, and it was beginning to look as if the hitherto most glorious reign of our history might end as the least. Gloom pervaded the halls and corridors of Versailles. Madame de Maintenon shivered by her fire in the coldest winter of record while her septuagenarian lord and master shook his head gravely over the latest dispatches. Throughout the icy palace makeshift chairs and tables had replaced the glorious silver furniture melted down to refill a depleted treasury.

It was at this, our lowest point, that the arrogance of our enemies turned the tide. Just as half the court were beginning to murmur about a negotiated peace, just as Madame de Maintenon herself, a shameless defeatist, was talking openly to her intimates about the advisability of Philippe V's abdicating, news came of the proposed allied conditions. Not only should our king have to expel from his court the exiled Stuart pretender; he should have to assist actively in the dethroning of his own grandson! Versailles, Paris, all of

France were suddenly united in a single resolution. From the highest rank to the lowest the nation rallied behind the embattled old monarch and flung down the gauntlet before the allied powers. Out of defeat we were to snatch, if not victory, then a kind of stalemate.

But behind our new unity there was, at least at court, a deep and dangerous division. Although the king was still in good health, it was beginning to be obvious, even to those most in awe of him, that he could not live forever, and it is in the nature of courtiers to look to the new reign. The powers at Versailles were split into two factions: those who hoped to dominate the dauphin when he should become Louis XV, and those who, knowing they had no chance of this, hoped at least to contain his power to harm them until *his* son should succeed, as Louis XVI. The dauphin, after all, was almost fifty, stupid, timid, overweight and over-indulgent. One knew the liability of such types to sudden strokes and seizures. His oldest son, the duc de Bourgogne, on the other hand, was strong, bright and virtuous. The little sympathy that existed between father and son required the ambitious courtier to make a choice between them — the issue could not be straddled. Did one want to be great in the brief and possibly inglorious reign of Louis XV or wait for the longer and presumably more splendid one of his successor?

The dauphin's cabal was centered at Meudon, the château near Versailles where he spent most of his days, avoiding as much as he could the magnificent sire who had always terrified him. He lived there with a plain little creature, a Mademoiselle Choin, whom he was supposed to have married after the death of the dauphine, but who was reputed to have little influence over him. The person who exercised this was none other than my old friend, his half-sister, Madame la Duchesse (de Bourbon), now widowed and seemingly intent on substituting the new pleasures of power for the old pleasures of the bed. She dazzled and fascinated the heir apparent, who did everything she wanted so long as she never asked him to give up a day's hunting, which, needless to say, she never did. Aiding her was the usual bevy of royal bastards: the dowager princesse de Conti (my late hero's sister-in-law), the duc du Maine and the comte de Toulouse.

Bourgogne, of course, was the center of the other faction, but, like his father, he did not dominate it. He was a noble prince, with a fine mind and high ideals, who had matured splendidly after a rather violent boyhood, but he was religious to the point of being priestly, and he was dreadfully inhibited with anyone of the least sophistication. His wife, who was all charm and loveliness, made up for his shyness as best she could, and held both the king and Madame de Maintenon in the palm of her hand, but she, too, lacked the force and self-confidence to dominate a faction of the court. For this there was only one person: the duc d'Orléans. Bourgogne trusted him, although deploring his irreligion, and liked to discuss with him the problems that would confront a new ruler. Orléans was not only a man of integrity; he had great intelligence, as I have previously emphasized, and he used the idleness that the king enforced upon him to study law, politics, military strategy and science. He even maintained a laboratory in the Palais-royal, where the smells and smokes of his experiments gave birth to widespread rumors that he was engaged in witchcraft!

The adherence of the duc and the duchesse d'Orléans to the Bourgognes had the effect, unfortunately, of deepening the rift between the latter and Meudon. But this could not be helped. When Orléans had at last — because of the grimness of the war situation — been given a command in Spain, he had incurred the undying wrath of Monseigneur (as the dauphin was known) by listening to a delegation of Spanish nobles who had come to suggest him as a possible successor to Philippe V. He had also, finally and fatally, dished himself with Madame de Maintenon by offering a toast to her at a drunken officers' dinner as "General Cunt, our true commander-in-chief." Of course, this was relayed to Versailles in a matter of days by galloping messengers. It was all most unfortunate, but I have made it clear in my memoirs that those who admired and liked Orléans (of whom I was always one) had to learn to put up with his occasional extravagances.

Between the two groups, or rather over them, was the perennial figure of the king and, at his side, that of Madame de Maintenon. Both adored the duchesse de Bourgogne, who was always with them, a kind of pet kitten, cajoling, joking, loving. Both were bored by the dauphin. On the other hand, the king regarded the too-pious Bourgogne as a bit of a prude or puritan, and he was always amused by Madame la Duchesse. And then, of course, Madame de Maintenon abominated Orléans and loved Maine. So wherever one looked one came up with a check or a balance. The factions were not unevenly weighted.

It was my conviction that a future sovereign who was in the hands of the bastards (except, of course, for the duchesse d'Orléans, who felt almost as I did about her co-illegitimates) would be the worst possible thing for the kingdom, and it was this that made me at last resolve to take up once more an active role in court intrigue. I felt that it was my duty to strengthen the party of the duc de Bourgogne: first, that it might find itself in a position to offer effective resistance to those who would be trying to dominate the new king, and second, that it might be ready to handle power when and if power should be available.

It should not come as a surprise to my reader at this point that it was Gabrielle who showed me where to start. This occurred in the salon of our little apartment, one morning, when she was ostensibly reading a volume of Madame de La Fayette and I was reviewing my weekly notes.

"The king wants to marry Berry," she said in a tone that was clearly intended to open a discussion.

"And high time. He's twenty-five." Charles, duc de Berry, the dauphin's third son, had moved closer to the succession when the second, the duc d'Anjou, had renounced his French rights on becoming king of Spain. "Who are the candidates?"

"Well, of course, the war makes it difficult to find a princess abroad." Gabrielle paused. I knew that she was perfectly sure of my attention. Neither of us would have to mention so obvious a fact as that the prospect of a home bride immediately presented the danger of a bastard. "I think that the duc d'Orléans should put up the name of Mademoiselle de Valois." This was the eldest Orléans daughter. She was only fifteen but reputedly mature for her age, and very handsome. I had not seen her for a year. "It would be just the thing to bolster Orléans with the king, with Bourgogne, with everyone of our persuason," Gabrielle continued. "And, what's more, Berry likes her."

I brushed this aside. "What about her bar sinister?"

"You mean her mother's? Don't you think that if you're pure Bourbon on your father's side, it makes up for being only a legitimated one on your mother's? After all, both the girl's grandfathers were sons of Louis XIII."

"I still point òut that if a son of that girl should ever sit on the throne, we should have a sovereign who was a great-grandson of Madame de Montespan by one of her lovers."

"But if that lover was the king?"

"What difference, genealogically, does it make *who* that lover was? Surely, Gabrielle, we've been over this a thousand times!"

"At least. Very well, you can choose. If the prize doesn't go to Mademoiselle de Valois, it will go to Mademoiselle de Bourbon."

"Are you sure of that?" I cried.

"Perfectly sure." Gabrielle's slightly puckered eyebrows showed that she appreciated my agitation. She liked to demonstrate her surer ear for court gossip. "Madame la Duchesse is pushing it for all she's worth. She's bound to pull it off if we don't act. *Now.*"

Well, here was a quandary. Madame la Duchesse's daughter was in precisely the same genealogical position as Mademoiselle de Valois. The girl's father, the late duc de Bourbon, was certainly a pure Bourbon, and her mother was only a legitimated one. Both girls were granddaughters of the king on the left-hand side.

"I suppose if it has to be one or the other," I mused, "one might as well pick the higher ranking: the daughter of a grandson of France as opposed to the daughter of a prince of the blood."

"Particularly when it's the Orléans against Madame la Duchesse!"

We agreed at length that Gabrielle should speak that very day to the duchesse d'Orléans, and I to her husband. Gabrielle, I had to admit again, did better than I. Madame Lucifer threw her pride to the winds and confessed eagerly to my wife how ardently she desired the match. She even promised Gabrielle the position of lady of honor to the new duchesse de Berry if the match came off. I at once demurred to this.

"Your rank entitles you to be lady of honor to the duchesse de Bourgogne!"

"But that position is filled."

"We can afford to wait."

Gabrielle hesitated. When she hesitated, I knew I was being "managed." "We can talk about it later," she said. "*If* we pull this off."

I had no trouble about the duc d'Orléans agreeing to the proposal. He adored his oldest child, almost at the expense of his other children; they had had, the two of them, father and daughter, from her earliest years, an extraordinary compatibility of wit and temperament, and it was natural that he should want for her the greatest match in the land, which Berry (Bourgogne's son being but an infant) still was. But he showed an unexpected reluctance to go to the king himself.

"Why can't I just write him a letter?"

"You can. But you must hand it to him yourself."

"He makes me feel like a naughty schoolboy!"

"In many ways, sir, you *are* like a naughty schoolboy."

"Saint-Simon, I take a great deal from you!"

"Because you know it's for your own good."

At last the letter was written, and Orléans stood with it at the king's dinner, shifting it awkwardly from hand to hand, as he and

I watched that solitary royal eater at the spread table. When the king at last looked our way, I had actually to push my friend forward.

"Give me that letter, nephew," the king said gruffly. "I think I know what it contains. I shall give it my due consideration."

Afterwards, in the great gallery, Orléans and I embraced each other happily while everyone stared.

2

———◆———

MADAME LA DUCHESSE, though a widow, still occupied her great suite in the south wing. It was just like her to have persuaded the king, her father, not to make her vacate it for her son, the new duc de Bourbon. She turned to the usher who had opened the door for me.

"I shall receive nobody until I give you further word. Pray be seated, Monsieur de Saint-Simon." And now she served me with the fine silver platter of her total attention.

"We have so much in common, my dear duke," she began in that high, sad tone that she adopted when she wanted her hearer to think that, whatever her reputation for charm, for sophistication, for worldly wisdom, she was basically a disillusioned, faintly weary woman who knew what the real values were. "We have shared the tiny bit of gold to be found under the meretricious glitter of the court. Ah, yes, my friend, you and I have known good quality. I sometimes wonder how you can put up with all the tawdriness that my sister considers 'royal tone' at the Palais-royal. And, to be quite frank, how *I* can put up with some of the nonsense that goes on at Meudon."

"Is there so much nonsense at Meudon?" I demanded, moving at once to the offensive. "I thought it was all so serious there."

"You mean that the Choin is training to be as great a prude as my 'stepmother'? Well, there might be something in that. But, poor dear, she has none of Madame de Maintenon's brains. Take it from me, if my brother ever reigns in this land, she will play a very small role."

"If she takes a certain sister-in-law's advice."

"And she will, duke, she will. I have put her where she is, and she is very grateful for it. I may be in a position to put other people in other places. *If* I can count on their gratitude."

I always had to admire the way Madame la Duchesse made use of the appearance of candor. She seemed to be placing herself with a fine courage, or even with a certain splendid indifference, entirely in your hands. But I knew perfectly well that if I should ever report her remarks back to Mademoiselle Choin, how quickly and effectively she would repudiate them! I could almost hear her ringing denial to the dauphin's indignant spouse: "Is it likely, my dear, that if I were inclined to spread such abysmal stories about you, I should take them to the one man who would be bound to betray me? Don't you know that Saint-Simon is Orléans' minion? Or would be if that were not the sole vice that my brother-in-law eschews?" Yes, *that* was how she would talk!

"Well, that will be very agreeable for those of your friends who are possessed of ambition," I replied, returning to her hint of promotion. "Unfortunately for me, I have none. I am perfectly content with my humble role at court."

"But does Gabrielle share this new love of obscurity? Where did I get the idea that she would not take it amiss to be appointed lady of honor to a daughter of France?"

"There are only two such. Gabrielle is too young for Madame, and the duchesse de Bourgogne has her lady already."

Madame la Duchesse allowed her stare to become searching. "The duc de Berry may marry."

"I should think that Gabrielle might find his spouse too young."

"She would need training the more."

"It would be an exhausting post. My wife has many domestic duties."

Madame la Duchesse must have now realized that the Orléans

had already offered us the post. She would have to try another lure.

"You and I don't have to beat about the bush. We both know that Orléans is in Madame de Maintenon's bad books because of that tactless little toast in Spain. If he would really like to get back in her graces, he could hardly do better than make a friend of me."

"I was under the impression that he had done just that."

"Lovers, my dear duke, are not necessarily friends. Oh, you needn't purse your lips like that! We don't have to pretend that *you* don't know all about me. Everyone is aware that Orléans is always boasting about what he's an ass enough to consider his conquests. But if he would spend less time making love — if that's the word for what he does — and more making friends . . . well, there might be things I could do for him."

"You could make Madame de Maintenon *like* him?"

"That's a tall order, I admit," she replied, with a frank laugh. "But I think I could convince her that what he said about her in Spain was simply what he says about *all* our sex. Madame de Maintenon has always had a bit of a weakness for me. She cares about unity in the royal family, and if I told her I could bring it about . . . well, who knows what I might not accomplish?"

I considered this coolly. Did Madame la Duchesse think me such a fool as to renounce the Berry marriage for a few useless good words put in with an old woman who was an implacable enemy of Orléans? No. She was covering a threat, and she expected me to see it. But I played dumb.

"I'm sorry, but I fear that the duc d'Orléans has fallen into such low esteem with Madame de Maintenon that even your amiable offices would not suffice to pull him out."

Madame la Duchesse at this threw me a harder look. "Very well, Monsieur de Saint-Simon. Let me put it this way. Your friend Orléans has made some very grave enemies at court. He may wake up some day to find that one of them has become his sovereign. Are you aware that there are people in the dauphin's immediate entourage who go so far as to label Orléans' conduct in Spain treason? And who believe that he should stand trial for it?"

"I am so aware, ma'am. But the charges at the very worst amount to no more than that he permitted himself to listen to certain grandees who asked him to consider the Spanish crown if Philippe V should abdicate. There is no treason to the king of France in discussing, while in Spain, a question of the Spanish succession."

"Even when the king of France has crowned the king of Spain? Even when they are grandfather and grandson?"

"That, ma'am, must be deemed in law a mere coincidence. And surely Monseigneur, should he become our sovereign, would not strain the law more than his own father has done!"

I had her there. She would have to unsheathe her sword. *If* she had one.

"Monseigneur, if ever called to the throne, will be, I am confident, a very great king. But he is no better a prince than a father, sir. His devotion to his three sons, and in particular to the youngest, is touching to see. He will naturally be intensely interested in the character of the bride selected for the duc de Berry. Particularly as Berry himself, however charming and handsome a youth, is of a singular naïveté."

"Naïve in what respect?"

"Naïve in taking for purest gold what may have a sizable quantity of alloy. For seeing as innocent and virginal, for example, a princess who may have considerably more experience than he imagines." Here Madame la Duchesse paused menacingly. "Experience, indeed, of what I fear may be an appalling nature."

"To what do you allude, ma'am?"

"I think I shall leave that to you to find out," she said finally. "It should not be difficult." She raised her voice now to tell her usher that she would receive.

I was perplexed. Obviously, Madame la Duchesse knew something about Mademoiselle de Valois that I didn't but that she was convinced I did. I took my departure and went to our apartment, where I found Gabrielle dressing for mass. When I gave her my account of the interview she regarded my image curiously in her mirror.

"Don't you know what it is?" she asked.

"Why should I not tell you if I did?" I asked, with some pique.

"Because you were shocked. Or because you were afraid to shock me."

"Is it so bad then?"

"Pretty bad." She paused and fixed her gaze again on my reflection. "Madame la Duchesse is referring to the rumor that the duc d'Orléans and Mademoiselle de Valois are lovers."

"Orléans! With his own daughter! That *child!* Oh, come, Gabrielle, even Versailles can't be so obscene!"

"Can't it? You should know better. There's nothing people won't say."

"But can any of them really believe it?"

"Of course they can really believe it. Once a thing's said, it's bound to be believed."

I hesitated. "Surely *you* don't believe it?"

There was a pause, during which Gabrielle looked down at her brushes and combs. They were ancient pieces, of heavy silver, with gorgons' heads and warriors, which had belonged to my father's mother. Gabrielle's delay made the air in our chamber seem heavy, as with some malign incense. "I don't go in for belief or disbelief," she said at last. "I simply make a point of noting what is said."

I was exasperated by her calm. "You mean you don't really mind — it doesn't appall you — it doesn't make your blood run cold that a father as devoted as Orléans should actually seduce his fifteen-year-old child? I mean, the mere idea of it, Gabrielle! Of course, I shouldn't like even to sully my lips by denying it. Good God!"

I stopped. The words seemed to have choked me. Gabrielle was brushing her hair, having sent away her maid when I came in. The long, hard strokes and her intent gaze into the mirror seemed to imply that my protests were simply the kind of thing that a woman had to put up with in court, like the overcrowding in the receptions and the bad smell in the corridors. That incest in the royal family should be a fact or a rumor; that the idea of it should titillate some people and horrify others; these were simply aspects of a piece of news at the palace that it was Gabrielle's duty, or pastime, or perhaps even her pleasure, to sift and classify. Did it matter if it was true or not? Did not its existence in the minds of the courtiers give it a kind of truth, perhaps even an adequate truth?

"Look, my dear," Gabrielle said at last, turning to me as with a desire to be reasonable. "Let us not get into a dispute about incest. I am perfectly willing to concede it is a mortal sin. That is a matter for God. The matter for us is what Madame la Duchesse is planning to do with this weapon. It seems obvious to me that what she was trying to tell you was that she will take it to the king if the Orléans do not at once withdraw from the Berry marriage."

"You mean the king doesn't *know*? Isn't that kind of gossip relayed to him immediately?"

"Not necessarily. There are some things people are afraid to tell him. Remember the messengers of bad news who, in ancient days, were put to death. I, for one, should think twice before imparting to his majesty the unwelcome information that there was incest in his family. And that his only nephew is proposing a child of his, whom he has seduced, the king's granddaughter to boot, as the unsoiled bride of the king's grandson!"

"But I thought the king's police spies had to tell him everything!"

"Well, suppose they did. Would he believe them? What Madame la Duchesse will do is *prove* it to him."

I gaped. "Prove it to him?"

"You know she has a way of making her stories stick. Even when her father doesn't trust her and knows that she has a motive for lying. The woman has an absolute genius for invention. And then, too, she will make the thing seem so real that, even if she isn't entirely believed, Mademoiselle de Valois will be hopelessly soiled in the king's eyes. It doesn't, after all, take much, and the child has a very lively personality for her age."

"What can we do then?" I asked in despair.

"Fight fire with fire," Gabrielle replied promptly. "Or, better yet, get to the king before Madame la Duchesse. Tell him about her affair with Monseigneur!"

Had I heard this before the Orléans story, I should have been shocked inded. But I was now too numb, hardened already to the royal world that Gabrielle was opening up to me.

"With her own brother?" I asked weakly.

"With her half-brother," Gabrielle corrected me. "But it will be equally horrible to the king. They're equally his children, after all. And, unlike Orléans and the little Valois, it's more than a rumor. It's gospel truth!"

"What do you mean, Gabrielle, by gospel truth?" I asked gravely.

"I mean that I had it from the dowager princesse de Conti, who had it from Mademoiselle Choin herself. That poor creature is absolutely terrified of Madame la Duchesse, who tells her that the dauphin will repudiate her unless she acts as a cover to their intrigue. Of course, it's perfectly true that he's tired of the Choin, and that she owes her marriage entirely to Madame la Duchesse, who wanted to keep her brother from marrying a possible rival, so the Choin has no weapon to use. When Monseigneur goes to her bedroom, the wretched morganatic spouse must shiver in the closet while Madame la Duchesse, slipping in by a side door, wantons in the arms of her portly sibling!"

Gabrielle saw that I was now hypnotized and took full advantage of it. I had never heard her speak so cuttingly or, for that matter, so vividly.

"But the dauphin is a religious fanatic!" I protested. "He's even superstitious. How does he expect to save his immortal soul?"

"Ah, that's where Madame la Duchesse is at her smartest. She has persuaded him that she can get him a dispensation. She's used her mother's old magic tricks. Incantations, formulas, who knows? Maybe even a black mass. The poor dauphin's fascinated by her wickedness. He probably finds it sexually stimulating! He's besotted with her. And he has to do everything she says, or she'll withdraw the charm, and then he'll go straight to hell when he dies!"

"Where they both deserve to go," I retorted in disgust.

"Well, do you think the king will want Mademoiselle de Bourbon for Berry when he hears all *that?*"

"She's just as much his granddaughter as Mademoiselle de Valois."

"Perhaps doubly so!" Gabrielle exclaimed with a sharp little laugh. "How do we know how long this affair with Monseigneur has been going on?"

I threw up my hands in a final expression of dismay. "I must go to the Palais-royal," I told her now. "I must have this out with Orléans. The whole wretched thing!"

3

---◆---

IN MY LETTER to the duc d'Orléans, I did not mince my words.
I described in full detail my interview with Madame la
Duchesse and then outlined Gabrielle's information and proposal.
I told him that I should wait on him the following day at the Palais-
royal and request his permission to approach the king through the
duchesse de Bourgogne. This last had also been Gabrielle's idea.
The duchesse de Bourgogne was not only the favorite of the king
and Madame de Maintenon; she was a daughter of Orléans' half-
sister (Monsieur's daughter by his first marriage, to Henrietta of
England) and she was very fond of her uncle. Even more important, she detested and feared the cabal of Meudon.

To my surprise, Savonne, when he heard that I was going to
the Palais-royal, offered to accompany me. He and I had to some
degree patched up our old friendship, after the Polish fiasco, when
Gabrielle had convinced him that she alone was to blame, but
the relationship had never been the same. He had given up any
idea of taking religious orders, and I disapproved of his dissolute
bachelor's life. He was privy to our project of the Berry-Orléans
marriage, and professed to approve of it, but I had not trusted him
with Gabrielle's plan.

"But I shall have to talk to Orléans alone," I pointed out.

"That's all right. I can pay my respects to the duchess. And to
Mademoiselle de Valois."

"Mademoiselle de Valois? She's only a child."

"You haven't seen her for a while. She's developed. She's charming."

"Oh, very well. Come along."

It occurred to me on the drive into Paris that it was odd that Savonne should be showing so little desire to rejoin his regiment, from which he had obtained an indefinite leave. Some people thought he was courting the youngest Mademoiselle de Beauvillier, and indeed it was high time, at thirty-seven, that he should marry, but the old duke had not spoken to me about the possibility of such a match, and I was almost certain that he would have. I considered it more likely that Savonne was deep in some adulterous intrigue. Never in my wildest dreams did I suspect the truth.

We were waiting for the duchesse d'Orléans in the great portrait gallery when the door at the far end burst open and a young woman, or a girl, it appeared, came running across the floor to us. I stared at such unseemly behavior, but I stared a good deal harder when I realized that it was Mademoiselle de Valois herself.

"Monsieur de Savonne!" she exclaimed, as she pulled up, panting, before us. "I heard you were here. Why did you not ask for me? How dare you come to the Palais-royal without asking for me?"

I looked in amazement at my friend, who had turned very red. I had had no idea that he was on such terms with a princess who was young enough to have been his daughter. And where, for that matter, was the princess's governess?

"I would not have presumed," Savonne murmured, bowing to her. "I had no idea . . . I could not tell that . . ." He paused and looked at me in embarrassment, for all the world like a boy caught in some silly prank.

"Do you think, because I shall be duchesse de Berry, that I am to have no friends of my own?" the little lady continued imperiously. "Tell him, Monsieur de Saint-Simon, that the court is not like that!"

I was struck dumb. Could this radiant, flashing-eyed blonde be only fifteen? She had certainly, in the year since I had last seen her, turned into a beauty. She moved, she laughed, she gesticulated, like her aunt Madame la Duchesse. She was small but perfectly formed, and conveyed a sharp sense of vitality. As I watched her turning her wiles on poor Savonne, I suddenly had a vision of this girl with her father, and my mind went dark.

"I had not been aware that you and Monsieur de Savonne were such friends," I managed to murmur.

"Oh my, yes!" she replied. "He has been frequently at Saint-Cloud. He has given me riding lessons. We have fished in the stream. Monsieur de Savonne is much acquainted with the great out-of-doors. When I am married I shall join the king's hunt, and Monsieur de Savonne will accompany me."

"He will be much honored, I am sure," I observed, giving my speechless friend a glance. "But tell me, Mademoiselle, has something happened to your lady-in-waiting? I am sure your father would be distressed to have you so unattended in his house."

"I am attended as I desire to be, Monsieur de Saint-Simon," she replied in a lofty tone. "I am only surprised that you should comment on it."

"The duke allows more latitude here than at Versailles," Savonne put in, happy to change the topic from himself. "He has advanced ideas for the education of princesses."

"I see."

"Which means you don't," Savonne retorted, taking refuge in the offensive. "Of course, we know that you think everything should be done as it was in the days of Charlemagne. It may interest you to know that Mademoiselle de Valois studies the heavenly bodies at night through her father's telescope and aids him with experiments in his laboratory."

"I have no objection to learning in a princess," I retorted. "But I do not know what *your* qualifications are in that respect. Now that Mademoiselle can ride and fish, perhaps she will graduate to more sophisticated instructors."

"Oh, but Savonne is a *friend!*" the impertinent chit exclaimed. "I do not rank him with my tutors. He, like you, is helping to make my marriage!"

"I was aware of that." I gave Savonne another stare. "But I did not realize, perhaps, at what cost to his personal feelings."

Mademoiselle gave a little shriek of laughter. "Oh, he knows I couldn't marry *him!* So he naturally wants what's best for me. I should, I suppose, be marrying a crowned head, but what girl wants to leave France? Think of my poor aunt, who died a queen in Madrid, chained in etiquette. They say she was poisoned, but I'm sure she died of boredom. No, it's better to be a princess at Versailles than a queen anywhere else. As duchesse de Berry, I shall be the second lady of France. I shall outrank my mother and grandmother!"

I found at last that I was able to adjust to this new view of Mademoiselle de Valois. After all, she was a granddaughter of Madame de Montespan, and the Mortemarts were famous for their precocity, worldliness and wit. But what still remained as a shock was my sense of Savonne's involvement. He was staring at this young creature with positively watery eyes!

"The greater the rank, the greater the responsibilities," I warned her. "And I do not consider that our etiquette is as much laxer than that of Spain as you suppose. Consider the king himself."

"Oh, but he *likes* etiquette," she said with a sniff. "That's different. I shall like it myself. At certain times. Oh, yes, I'm like *you,* Monsieur de Saint-Simon. My father has even compared me with you. He says that you and I know all the rules. But one has to know the rules to know how to get around them. Look at the duchesse de Bourgogne. *She* does."

I was about to defend her future sister-in-law from this imputation (although there *had* been rumors there — God knew how this girl had got wind of them!), when both wings of the central door were thrown open and the duchesse d'Orléans entered, followed by two of her ladies. She was as fair as her daughter and of almost as smooth a complexion, but she was much taller and more statuesque.

"Elizabeth!" she said sternly. "You are not to receive gentlemen alone. I have told you that repeatedly."

"I am not receiving anyone, Mama. I simply found these gentlemen here. I suppose I may walk about my own home as I please?" Mademoiselle de Valois' tone certainly did not show the slightest awe of her mother. She turned to me now as if the latter had not been present. "Of course, you noticed, Monsieur de Saint-Simon, that *both* doors were opened for the duchess. I do not suppose she would expect such a courtesy at Versailles, where it is reserved exclusively for the children of France. My father, as a grandson, does not claim it, even here. But Mama maintains, at least in her own domain, that a legitimated child of France ranks with a real one."

"You are insolent!" cried the duchess. "Leave us!"

Her daughter continued to talk to me without offering her mother the slightest attention. "When I have my own apartment at Versailles, as duchesse de Berry, you may be sure that only *one* door of my salon will be opened for Mama. The double accolade will be reserved for myself, for my husband, for my grandmother, for the dauphin and for the duc and duchesse de Bourgogne. You see, Monsieur de Saint-Simon, I *have* learned the rules!"

"You are not duchesse de Berry yet," the duchess reminded her tartly. "*That* chicken should not be counted until it's hatched. Will you leave us, Mademoiselle?"

"Come, Savonne!" Mademoiselle de Valois called to him. "I want to show you my new portrait by Monsieur Rigaud. It is considered his finest."

As she walked quickly away, followed by the subservient Savonne, the duchess turned to one of her ladies.

"Go with her and *stay* with her." As the lady hurried off to obey, the duchess addressed me. "My dear old friend, the duke is waiting for you in his laboratory. But I want to have a word with you first." Her other lady discreetly drew back, and Madame d'Orléans and I strolled together up and down the great empty chamber.

"Poor Berry," she said, "he will have his hands full if he marries her. He's a most amiable and attractive young man, but he's short on brains, and she's going to lead him around with a ring through his nose. It doesn't make it any better that he's already crazy about her."

"Like Savonne," I said grimly.

"Oh, like half the men she meets," the duchess agreed readily. "Savonne is just another convenient slave. There's nothing I or her grandmother can do with her. Of course, it's my husband's fault. He lets her get away with everything. There's never been so indulgent a father."

I paused to glance at her. "So I gather."

She returned my look without blinking. "That's what I wished to discuss with you. The rumor of which you quite properly informed us is without the smallest basis in fact."

"Dear Madame, you don't have to tell me that!"

"Ah, but I do. Every such rumor must be strenuously denied. To everyone." Here she actually condescended, great proud princess though she was, to place her arm under mine as we continued our stroll. "There is a nasty little something in all of us that tends to credit the vilest stories about our nearest and dearest. At first we stare and violently shake our heads. How too dreadful even to be thought of! And then we begin to reflect. A very little bit of reflection goes a long way. After all, is it so impossible? Wasn't he — or she — always somewhat inclined to . . . oh, yes, let's face it. Hadn't we even suspected it?"

"I never did!"

"Well, God bless you, I'm sure you didn't. But others have. So I know I must deny it. And here and now I do!" She took her hand from my arm and raised it, as if to affirm an oath. "I have had to put up with a great many infidelities from my husband. Nobody knows that better than you, my friend. But I have never forgotten that he was married to me against his will and that he has always tried to be kind to me. I have loved him for that, and I shall always love him. He is a man of high character. Had he been capable of the things you wrote to us about, I should have known!"

At that moment I forgave her all her airs and vanities, all her pretensions and ambitions. She was no longer "legitimated"; she had become to me, at least, legitimate. I dropped to one knee and kissed her hand.

"But as to the other rumor," she continued, with a sudden flush, "the one about my sister and the dauphin, I believe it absolutely! And please, for the sake of my husband, for the sake of my daughter, for the sake of France, persuade the duke to make use of it!"

I nodded devoutly and took my leave of her, to find Orléans in his laboratory. This chamber, although paneled and decorated like the other rooms in the palace, was marred — at least to my vision — by a long trestle table on which stood some dozens of glass tubes and large, opened folios. Orléans was peering into a basin when I entered.

"I am studying the breathing of a frog," he said, turning to face me. "It occurred to me that . . ." And then he stopped, observing my expression of distaste. "Oh, very well, I know you consider this unworthy of a prince. I should concern myself more with the delightful topics discussed at court. Fathers who sleep with their daughters. Sisters who sleep with their brothers."

"These things were not of *my* invention," I protested.

"No, of course not. But if we touch them, are we not defiled?"

"All I ask is that you let me handle the matter for you."

"And leave me clean? Leave me pure?"

"Why not?"

"What of the king? How will he react to these revelations?"

"That will be the concern of the duchesse de Bourbon."

"I care nothing about her. Or even about the dauphin. But I care about my uncle. Is this a time to burden him with further worries?"

"With all due respect, sir, I suggest that the king is not a sensitive man. He will be perfectly unaffected."

"Ah, you don't know him!" Orléans turned from his work table now and guided me to a corner where there were two large *ber-gères*. "I decided, when I heard you were coming today, that I should have to tell you a story."

"And what story is that?"

"Sit down and let me pour you a glass of wine. I want to tell you about myself and the king. Things that even *you* don't know, Monsieur de Saint-Simon!"

4

WHAT YOU must try to understand, Saint-Simon, is that my father was only part of a family tragedy. The other, the much larger part of it, was the king. Think of those two lonely little boys at four and two, one the mightiest of monarchs (or so people told him); the other, his heir. Of course they had a mother, but my grandmother was entranced and preoccupied with her delightful new position as queen-regent, bowed to and flattered by everybody, an elevation all the headier for having been preceded by twenty years of neglect and humiliation, years in which she had been ignored by her husband, bullied by his iron cardinal, taunted for her long infertility and even menaced with exile.

So all was sudden heaven for Queen Anne in 1643. A pesky spouse was dead; an officious Richelieu was dead; a beautiful kingdom was in her hands; and she was not too old — at forty-two — to enjoy it all to the full. As for the two little boys, well, were there not enough people to look after them, hundreds and hundreds of people? And Giulio Mazarini was so handsome, so vigorous, so beguiling. I have always wondered if he didn't marry my grandmother. After all, he was only a cardinal, not a priest. He perfectly well could have.

Even the Fronde did not altogether spoil Queen Anne's fun. I think in some ways it may have even enhanced it. There must have been romance in the excitement, the bustle, the rushing from castle to castle, the appealing to armies, a beautiful, harassed widow clutching her two infants to her side. And Mazarin was there, always there, to support her, to love her, to make the plans, to take the blame.

When it was over, and she had made him, or allowed him to make himself, the master of France, he turned his attention to her sons. Acting, let us presume, for the sake of his soul, if he had one, in what he deemed the best interests of the nation, but proceeding to his goal with the deliberation and ruthlessness of his fellow countryman Machiavelli, he set about the task of turning the elder boy into a great king and the younger into a creature who would never rival a great king. Richelieu, his preceptor, had taught him what a thorn in the side Gaston d'Orléans had been to Louis XIII. This could not be allowed to happen again.

And so, while my uncle was trained with arms and exercises, my father was encouraged to sniff scents and play with jewelry. One was encouraged to believe that beautiful women had been created only for his lust; the other was surrounded with pretty boys coached in vice. The plan worked. If my uncle became a monster of egotism, he also became strong and disciplined, perhaps the most perfect prince ever reared and trained for a throne. My poor father, on the other hand, became . . . well, you know only too well what he became. Yet even Mazarin was unable quite to keep his natural talents down. When Monsieur, after the cardinal's death, finally succeeded in obtaining a command in the field, he did so well that he had to be brought home!

The remarkable thing is that the two brothers always loved each other. I sometimes wonder if either of them ever really loved anyone else. It was as if, isolated by their rank from the rest of the world, fatherless and, as I have explained, almost motherless, they recognized that what was being done to them would have been, had their ages been reversed, itself reversed; that they had only themselves to cling to and to trust in a universe that, for its own arcane reasons, had to put them in gilt cages and stare at them and, from time to time, even poke at them through the bars.

Oh, I know, of course, that the king adored Marie Mancini and that he had a kind of passion for the Vallière and the Montespan, and I suppose you might say that Monsieur loved the Chevalier. But those were matters of Eros. Do you suppose the king ever loved his own children or grandchildren? You have seen how he is with them. He likes to have them constantly about him, and he is perfectly willing to give them money and honors, but he never allows intimacies, and they're all in holy terror of him, except the little duchesse de Bourgogne, and she's treated more like a kitten than a grandchild. And my father, although he was friendly and gregarious, was basically as reserved as his brother. It was only when you saw him joking or quarreling with the king that you had a sense that they were both human beings with a human bond between them.

Unless there was something of one between Monsieur and myself. I think he wanted it; I know that I did. But he was always afraid that I was going to be shocked by his sex life. He was glad, I believe, that I did not share his inclinations, but it still made him shy with me. I think our first intimate moment came when he took up my defense with Mother after she discovered that, at the age of fifteen, I had impregnated one of her chambermaids.

Had this happened at Versailles or with a member of my father's household, it would have been only an occasion for lewd jokes or even congratulations. But Mother had a Germanic prudishness and set great store by the virtue of her retainers. The poor girl was shown the gate, and I had my ears soundly boxed. You will remember, Saint-Simon, that Madame maintained this practice right up until my marriage! And I'm not sure if I'm entirely safe to this day.

Monsieur took me aside and spoke to me with a gentleness I had not had from him before.

"Philippe, my dear, you are obviously a man now. And you're a man the way men should be. For all your mother's anger, she's basically proud of you. She has always dreaded that you might turn out . . . well, like somebody else. I never thought you would turn out other than you have. You will have the life I might have had. You will be happy, my boy, if I can make you happy. Bless you, my child!"

I burst into tears and threw my arms around him. It was the first time in my life that either of my parents had expressed so warm a concern. But there were other consequences of the chambermaid incident. When the Chevalier de Lorraine, attracted, no doubt, by the gossip of my sexual prowess, made a pass at me in the hall of armor, my one concern in resisting him was to do so in a way that no guards or ushers should observe. I placed one hand firmly over his lips and with the other twisted his arm behind his back.

"When I let you go, keep your mouth shut, you filthy pervert! If you try this again, I'll kill you. But Monsieur must never know. Is that clear?"

The Chevalier was smart enough to realize that I meant what I said. He had nothing to fear from me; I would never reveal to my father his aborted "infidelity." But his hatred was something that I had to be on my guard against right up to the day of my father's death.

Monsieur's behavior in respect to my marriage was typical of all that he tried and failed to do for me. He would approach the king about a command for me, or a governorship, or a foreign princess as a bride; he would set forth, in his nervous, excited fashion, all of his good reasons. The king would listen benignly, and Monsieur would come rushing back to me to tell me in exultation that he had carried his point. Time would pass, and nothing would happen. Monsieur would go again to the king and receive the famous, friendly "Have a chair, my brother." Then would follow the royal arguments, gravely and succinctly stated, against the particular proposition. Monsieur would raise his voice; Monsieur would even weep; but he never carried the day. The last argument that he had with the king, over my continued enforced idleness, brought on his fatal stroke.

Even after my father's death the king remained faithful to Mazarin's policy of keeping down the Orléans. Nothing would induce him to allow me to play a major role in the army or in the government. Nothing, that is, but dire necessity. The time at last came in this war when things were going so badly that he needed every available male of the blood royal at the different fronts to bolster morale, and I found myself at last in Spain. Well, my spirits were so exuberant that I drank too much at a military banquet at Madrid and made the famous toast that you know all about. That was bad enough, but worse was to follow: my unfortunate session with the grandees over the rumored abdication of Philippe V.

This is how it happened. It was in my tent, two days after my victory at Lérida. I was told of the arrival of a distinguished deputation, and I assumed that it was a visit of official congratulation. Victories in the Franco-Spanish army had been too few to be ignored. Well, you know how ceremonious our southern neighbors can be. It was only after an hour of soft harangues that I began to take in that we were discussing something other than my military prowess. It was actually being suggested that a possible basis for peace might be worked out with the substitution of myself for Philippe V on the Spanish throne! The argument was that England, Holland and the empire might be satisfied by the removal of a grandson of Louis XIV in favor of his nephew! The victory for them would be in obliging the king of France to rescind his initial act, which had caused the war. The face-saving for us would be that a French prince would still be king.

I listened, Saint-Simon. It was all I did. I listened because I was intrigued. Here at last was the unlooked-for chance of glory! Away from Versailles, away from France, what an opportunity for a new life, a new career! To say nothing of the occasion to lead a benighted old kingdom out of the dark ages in which it has more or less indolently lingered. Would I have been taking anything from my cousin, Philippe V, that he was not going to lose anyway? Was it not even evident that the poor young man disliked the crown his grandfather had so remorselessly clamped on his reluctant head? Mightn't my uncle-father-in-law and I get on better as fellow sovereigns, with several hundred blessed miles between us? And why should I not be a king in Madrid? Was I not a great-grandson of Philippe IV and a half-brother of the unhappy, late lamented Queen Marie-Louise?

Well, of course, it all looked very different to Versailles. Monseigneur was livid. He told his father that I was planning to assassinate his son. Madame de Maintenon, recalling my infamous toast, made the welkin ring with her complaints. Ugliest of all was the charge that, as a French general, I had been disloyal to my commander-in-chief. I was summoned home to report. The dreaded word "treason" was on every tongue.

I confess I did not know what to expect. My wife was very fine. She brushed aside the long history of my infidelities and appeared everywhere at my side. She said she would go to her father, but I knew how little the king was swayed by his daughters. I found myself shunned by all. My very appearance at a chamber at Versailles was enough to send people flying to doors and corners. And then I was told that the king would see me. Alone.

When the doors of his study were closed, he rose and approached me. He was serious, but not severe.

"My nephew," he said gravely, "I have read all the reports. I know that you listened to treasonable talk. It was very foolish of you, but it was only that. You have many vices, my friend, but there is no disloyalty in your nature, as there was none in your father's. You and I have had our differences. No doubt you have found me harsh, even cruel. It is not easy to be a monarch. But I do only what I think I must do. I have never been swayed by affection or by dislike from the performance of my duties." Now he even smiled! "I should not trust you, sir, with a young wife if I had one, but I trust you absolutely as a soldier and as a friend!"

Well, what would *you* have done, Saint-Simon? I fell to my knees and wept. And do you think now, in the midst of a terrible war, with every sword in Europe pointing at that old man's heart, I'm going to add to his woes by shrill complaints about his daughter and his heir?

5

MONSEIGNEUR rarely came to a Marly weekend. Mademoiselle Choin was not welcome there, as the presence together of the two morganatic spouses of the two highest men of the land might have given rise to some degree of smothered hilarity. The awe and dignity of Madame de Maintenon's position depended on its uniqueness; having no rank in a court of rigid hierarchies gave her a detachment, an isolation and, ultimately, an elevation, that were superior to the very grandest title. But if there were two of them, they would constitute a kind of class, and a class would have to be ranked, and theirs would not be the first.

The dauphin was a stout, stupid, occasionally amiable man, with a remarkable memory for trivia in the few areas of life that interested him. He could, for example, and would, alas, insist on telling you precisely how many stags, how many boars, even how many pheasants had been killed in the royal hunts over the past decade, contrasting the number at Versailles with that at Fontainebleau and with that at Chambord, and ascribing to the variations all kinds of tiresome reasons. He had been fond of his three sons, but since Bourgogne had been drawn by his wife into Madame de Maintenon's camp and Anjou had gone to Spain, he had been reduced, as an affectionate parent, pretty much to Berry, a big, handsome, friendly young man, without a brain in his head, who also lived to hunt.

At the important Marly weekend to which I now address myself,

Monseigneur was present, as were Berry and Madame la Duchesse (de Bourbon). The candidacy of Mademoiselle de Valois was now being openly discussed, and the dauphin made no effort to conceal his strong disapproval of it. In the presence of the king he was, as always, mute and ill at ease, a gawky, foot-shifting, fifty-year-old schoolboy. But away from the royal presence he could be explosively disagreeable, and it was my fate to feel the full brunt of his displeasure.

I was standing with a group of gentlemen in the billiard room, watching him finish a game with the duc de la Rochefoucauld. The dauphin, as usual, lost, which did not improve his temper, and as he turned away from the table, still holding his cue, he overheard, in the ostensibly casual chatter about the war in Spain, some gentleman, obviously trying to "draw" him, state that the duc d'Orléans should be sent back to the front.

"Do you think so, sir? Do you indeed?" Monseigneur demanded, brandishing his cue like a weapon. "And why, pray, do you think any such thing?"

"Because he can win victories for France, Monseigneur."

"The devil himself can have luck," the dauphin retorted, with a stertorous grunt that was almost a belch. "But I think you will find that the king can see through a hollow victory like Lérida to the treason behind it!"

Our little group, delighted at this outburst, sought, by their feigned expressions of shock, to push the heir apparent to further indiscretions.

"Treason!"

"What can Monseigneur mean by that?"

"Surely, sir, you do not refer to your cousin of Orléans?"

Only poor Berry seemed genuinely upset. He was, after all, already half in love with Mademoiselle de Valois. "Oh, Father, treason," he stammered, "isn't that . . . well . . . isn't that going a bit far?"

"Well, what better word would *you* choose?" his father demanded in exasperation. "He wanted your brother's crown for himself, didn't he?" Here, turning back to the billiard table to fling his cue upon it, he encountered my eye and immediately stiffened. "Did he not, Monsieur de Saint-Simon?" he called challengingly.

"I believe, sir, that the king interpreted his nephew's behavior more leniently."

"Did he so? Did he indeed? Well, of course, the king makes every effort to see members of his family in a charitable light. But that only increases the duty of his family to see that his charity does not expose him to treachery. And in this case I have a duty to *two* sovereigns." He looked around the group in his most comically haughty manner. He might have been a caricature of his father. "After all, gentlemen, am I not the only prince in Europe who can describe two living monarchs as 'the king my father' and 'the king my son'?" A perfunctory murmur of admiration greeted this oft-repeated, rhetorical question. "The king of Spain and I, Monsieur de Saint-Simon, are in perfect accord in our interpretation of what happened at Lérida."

"I am only sorry that his majesty and your royal highness could not have been present at those conversations. I am confident that nothing was said that could have offended you."

"But you were not there, sir!"

"No, sir. But I believe implicitly in the honor and loyalty of your cousin and brother-in-law."

"In the loyalty and honor of an atheist!" Monseigneur exclaimed wrathfully, irked at my stress of the double relationship. "In the loyalty and honor of a man who spends his days in a heathen laboratory, playing with black magic, and his nights in debauchery! Monsieur de Saint-Simon, I can only say that you are either his dupe or his tool, and I will not insult you by calling you the latter!"

Tight-lipped and trembling with anger, I bowed and left the chamber. I hurried to our apartment, where I found Gabrielle. She showed little surprise when I told her what had happened.

"Very well, it's war," she said in clipped tones. "War to the death. Madame la Duchesse wants it, and Madame la Duchesse will get it. I'm going to Madame de Bourgogne. Be ready to join me there the moment I send for you."

"What will you do?"

"We must go over Orléans' head. There's no other way."

"But, Gabrielle, I gave him my word!"

"It's for his own good. He will understand. Believe me!"

When Gabrielle's usher came for me, half an hour later, I hurried to the Bourgognes' pavilion, and found myself in the presence of both duke and duchess. It was the first time that the four of us had been alone together.

Let me pause a moment to describe the man who might have been, had he lived, one of our greatest kings, and his enchanting consort. The duc de Bourgogne had a long, equine face and a short, stooped figure; the beauty of his young manhood, and beauty it was, seemed confined to his tensely glowing eyes and fine, pale forehead. He was serious, almost to a fault, determined to dedicate every hour to preparing himself for an earthly kingdom. It is our tragedy that a heavenly one should have pre-empted it. He never seemed to have even a minute to discuss anything but problems of government or religion. He would look at you blankly, even impatiently, if you attempted to talk to him of gossip or court matters, and then counter with a question such as: "But what will be the effect of the edict against monopoly on the carpet makers of Lille?" But if, like his grandfather, he had no small talk, he lacked altogether the king's royal demeanor. He was too nervous, too apologetic, too intense. We hoped that a more majestic air would come to him with time.

The duchess was just the opposite, except that her eyes wrought the same kind of enchantment that made one forget insignificant features and bad teeth. She was all charm, a charm that seemed to engulf other qualities, both good and bad, making them seem unnecessary, perhaps irrelevant. Thus it did not seem to matter that she was timid, frivolous, often inconsequential, almost a scatter-brain, or that her affections seemed almost too kittenish to be real. She was fond of her husband, who adored her with passion, but her smiles went everywhere, and there were those, malevolent I believe, who suggested that she sent more than smiles. In any event, she was so deeply embedded in the affections of the king and of Madame de Maintenon ("my aunt," she called the latter) that she had made herself — perhaps without any real design — a power at court.

The duke was pacing the chamber when I was admitted, seemingly very disturbed. He turned to me at once. "You know all about this, Monsieur de Saint-Simon? It is a fearful business. Your wife and mine think of it only as a means of preventing my brother's marriage to Mademoiselle de Bourbon, but I see it as affecting my father's soul!"

"But do the two things have to be mutually exclusive, my dear?" his wife inquired. "Surely the king, as soon as he is aware of it, will seek to discourage Monseigneur's connection with Madame la Duchesse. So we shall have killed two birds with one stone!"

"Particularly," Gabrielle put in, perhaps a bit too eagerly, "as a marriage between Mademoiselle de Bourbon and the duc de Berry would intensify the intimacy between her mother and Monseigneur."

Bourgogne gave Gabrielle a quick, sharp glance, as if to question her tact. But Gabrielle did not alter her expression. She stood her ground, motionless, her eyes cast downwards.

"How is the king to be told?" Bourgogne pursued. "I don't suppose *I'm* the one for that job."

"No, dear, of course not," the duchess replied soothingly. *"This* is peculiarly a woman's battle. Let me tell you how I propose to fight it."

"No, no, I'd rather not know!"

"Oh, but, my dearest, *yes,* or otherwise you will think that I've committed infamies! Listen to me — it's very simple. I shall pick a moment when I have persuaded Madame de Maintenon to spend an extra hour with the holy sisters at Saint-Cyr. That shouldn't be hard, as, poor dear, she's always craving more time there but doesn't dare leave the king. And, indeed, I'm the only person, for the moment, with whom she *can* leave him."

"Why can't you talk to him before Madame de Maintenon?" Bourgogne demanded.

"Because she hates Orléans so violently she'd swallow any horror on the other side."

"That's true, sir," I confirmed.

"So I must see the king alone," the duchesse de Bourgogne continued. "I shall get him started on the old days and his love for Marie Mancini. Oh, yes, he likes to talk about those things," she added, when she saw my look of surprise. "With *me,* anyway. He thinks me a wily but romantic Savoyard. Then I can touch on the matter of him and my own grandmother, the first Madame, and hint at his affair with her, which will introduce a note of the illicit, even the unnatural . . ."

"Marie-Adélaïde!" her husband protested in pain.

"We're making omelettes, my darling! We must be prepared to break a few eggs. I shall lead him lightly over some of the great amours of the court, gradually guiding him to the path of the unusual — or shall we say the bizarre? Until we come, quite naturally, to your father, my dear, and funny, fat little Mademoiselle Choin. Oh, I promise you, the king loves to laugh about *her.* And then it will be time, if all goes well, to put this candid question to him: 'In that respect, sire, my aunt de Conti' (he likes to have me refer to his bastards that way) 'used an expression the other day that surprised me. She spoke of the relationship between Monseigneur and my aunt de Bourbon as "romantic." Almost as if they were lovers. What do you suppose she could have meant by that?'"

"And that's all you'll say?" Bourgogne demanded.

"That's all I need say. He never lets anything drop. He'll call in the princesse de Conti, and she'll be on the spot. If she denies it, she'll have me to face, and the duchesse du Lude, who was with me when she said it."

"But why," I put in, "won't she simply get off the hook by saying that she was speaking hyperbolically? About a perfectly harmless relationship?"

"Because she won't want to!" Gabrielle responded now for the duchess. "She detests Madame la Duchesse for cutting her out with the dauphin. She hasn't dared tell the king, but she'll be only too happy to do so under the excuse of his cross-examination!"

The duke turned to me. "What do you say, Saint-Simon? Should we get mixed up in this kind of dirt?"

My heart was touched at the way he seemed to be drawing a line between the sexes. It was as if he were asking me to stand with him on the side of honor and decency and forbid our wives the subtle deviousness of what suddenly seemed an almost oriental court. But then I remembered the stertorous rudeness of the dauphin and the malicious eye of Madame la Duchesse.

"I'm afraid it's the only way, sir. I simply blush that our wives have had to show it to us."

6

THERE WAS a sense, some days later, throughout the corridors and reception chambers of Versailles, of a great piece of news about to break. Little groups of two or three stood about, nodding their heads gravely. Madame la Duchesse was seen storming out of Madame de Maintenon's room, haughty, defiant; and the dauphin, who had ordered his carriage for Meudon, was seen pacing back and forth in the Cour du Marbre, too impatient to wait until its arrival was announced to him. The duc and duchesse d'Orléans, coming from St.-Cloud, made no secret of their exhilaration. We walked, the three of us, in sprightly fashion about the parterre d'eau in full view of the courtiers who gawked at us from the windows of the great gallery.

"It's coming off!" the duchess said excitedly. "I know it's coming off!"

"Has the king told you so?" I asked.

"Of course not, but you know how he is. He has no confidences. He treats his children exactly the way he treats everyone else. But last night at the supper he asked me several questions about my daughter. Rather searching questions, I thought."

"And were your answers satisfactory to him?"

"As satisfactory as I could make them."

"You mean as satisfactory as wishful thinking could make them!" Orléans intervened with a burst of laughter. "Let us hope that darling Elizabeth will shape up! Which reminds me, my dear," he continued to his wife, "I must have a word with our old friend alone." And taking me by the elbow, he propelled me a few steps away from his wife, who now pretended to be absorbed in looking at the fountains. "Your friend Savonne," he said in a low voice. "Can you keep him away from court for a while? I can get him any army orders he wants."

"I can try. But why?"

"Don't you know?"

"But that was just a flirtation!"

"There are no flirtations at Versailles, Saint-Simon. You should know that. Get him away if you can. That's all I ask."

"You mean . . . you mean that Mademoiselle de Valois might refuse the duc de Berry because of Savonne!"

"No." Orléans' laugh was more like a little grunt. "She's too much of a Bourbon for that. It's he I'm worried about. He's such an ass. And an ass in love may do anything!"

I left him at once to find Savonne and take him for a walk in the orangerie. To my astonishment he made no secret of his passion for the little Valois and even claimed that it was returned! I was horrified.

"Then Orléans is right! You must go back to the army immediately!"

"It's obvious that you've never been in love," he said bitterly.

I let this pass. "It's obvious that I have a higher conception than you of our duty to the royal family!"

"Oh, stuff and nonsense. Everyone in the royal family sleeps with everyone else. Look at Madame la Duchesse. Look even at your sacred duchesse de Bour——"

"Hold your tongue!" I tried to put my hand over his mouth.

"Well, why don't you hold yours?" Savonne cried, breaking away from me. "I'm sick and tired of being bossed around by you!"

"You mean you have the gall to stand there and tell me that you intend to continue an intrigue with a princess who is about to become a daughter of France!"

"I mean that I'm a man, damn it all, and that as long as things are carried on in this court the way they *are* carried on, I see no reason why I should put a hundred miles between myself and the one creature in the world I've ever loved! Even if all I'm allowed to do is gaze at her when she walks behind the king to mass!"

There was something suddenly almost touching about poor Savonne as he blurted this out. He seemed only half his age: he seemed a good deal younger, indeed, than Mademoiselle de Valois. But I knew that I had to shock him into his senses.

"It is not only on such formal occasions that you would look upon her if you remain in court. You might be called upon to witness her accouchement of a grandchild of France. How would you like to see your beloved under *those* conditions?"

Savonne said nothing to this; he simply turned away, and I was struck by a nasty thought.

"Perhaps you think you might have a personal connection with the birth that would make the sight less unpleasant?" I asked sarcastically. "Let me remind you, my friend, how carefully the daughters of France are watched."

"Oh, Saint-Simon, you think you know everything!" he exclaimed in disgust. "But in a lot of ways you're very naïve. You've never gone in for love affairs, and you haven't learned that where there's a will, there's a way."

"A will!" I cried. "Do you mean to say you have a will to debase the blood royal of France? After all our talk, all our vows? I thought we were at least agreed on *that* principle. I thought we were united in the idea of the king and his true seed as the source of government under God! And now you're willing to risk engendering a child on the king's own granddaughter-in-law!"

"Well, anyway," Savonne growled, flushing, "my blood is as good as the king's! The Savonnes go back to Clovis!"

As I looked in stupefaction at the broad back that he now turned to me, I became aware of a scurry of feet on the gravel. It was a royal usher.

"Monsieur le duc de Saint-Simon!" he exclaimed, breathless. "The king desires your immediate presence. In the Garden of Apollo!"

I walked as fast as I could, without running, to the indicated spot. The king, as usual when he suffered from gout, was in his wheelchair, a bergère mounted on a platform with three small rollers, one in front, two in back, and covered by a palanquin. It was pushed by two deaf mutes, in scarlet, so that its occupant might enjoy security when talking as he was driven about. As I came up, the wheelchair moved forward, and I, but none of the encircling courtiers, followed.

"Monsieur de Saint-Simon," the king began in his rare amiable tone, "I consider that you have shown yourself a good friend to my family. There have been moments in the past, it is true, when I was somewhat less sure of that, but your good influence on my nephew, the duc d'Orléans, has more than made up for it. I consider that you have been a major factor in keeping his wildness under control, and that your good wife has contributed in no small degree to the harmony that exists between my daughter and him."

How impossible it is to convey the effect of those grave, measured tones! The king seemed never to stammer, never to be reduced, like the rest of us, to an "er" or an "ah." He chewed his words like his food, slowly and deliberately. Had I not had carefully to watch my step in keeping abreast of his chair, I should not for a moment have taken my fascinated gaze from those great glassy eyes. I attempted now to convey to the king some sense of the satisfaction that these compliments brought me, but he raised his hand to indicate that he wished to continue.

"I have always been aware that my nephew was a man of exceptional parts, and the time may well be near at hand when his advice and counsel will be needed by the state. I am an old man, Monsieur de Saint-Simon, and my son is not a young one. We must look to the future. That is why I am telling you how it gratifies me that you and the duchesse de Saint-Simon are on the terms that you are with the duc and duchesse d'Orléans. I am sure that you will be pleased to hear that I have decided to marry my granddaughter, Mademoiselle de Valois, to the duc de Berry."

I allowed my hands to come together in a little clap of joy. "Oh, sire, what a wise and wonderful match!"

"There had been," the king continued, giving no heed to my explosion, "some consideration of a union between the duc de Berry and another granddaughter of mine, but this seemed too good an occasion to tighten our ties with the House of Orléans. Now let me explain where all this concerns *you*." My heart suddenly sank as I saw the direction his next words were taking. "Mademoiselle de Valois has a lively personality and strong enthusiasms. While these can be assets in a princess, they can also, if not controlled, become liabilities. My grandson is amiable and affectionate but far too trusting. He will easily fall under his wife's influence. I must have, as her lady of honor, someone whom I can absolutely trust to keep her in line. The lady I propose is Madame la duchesse de Saint-Simon!"

It was all I could do to keep from reeling. So this was where all my dreams and ambitions and loyalties were to end up: that I should be the consort of the lady of honor to a child of a bastard! That I should bow my knee to, place the seal of my arms on, the very system that had ben my peculiar abomination!

"If you will pardon me, sire, for even hesitating in the face of so great and undeserved an honor, would it be presumptuous of me to inquire if the rank of the duchesse de Saint-Simon does not entitle her to be lady of honor to the duchesse de Bourgogne?"

"But that position is already filled," the king answered easily. "If the duchesse du Lude should ever relinquish it, it would be time enough to consider your wife's qualifications." Oh, yes, he had thought it all out. He knew he had me!

"Would it be possible, sire, for me to have twenty-four hours in which to consult my wife?"

"But that's quite unnecessary, my dear fellow. Madame de

Maintenon has already done so and finds her delighted to accept the post. Madame de Maintenon, I do not hide from you, had favored the candidacy of Mademoiselle de Bourbon to marry Berry. One of the conditions of her change of mind was that Madame de Saint-Simon should head the Berry household. So there you are. It all depends on you!"

Of course, I knew it didn't. But when such a king as Louis XIV professed to ask your permission to marry two of his grandchildren to each other, what did you do? The valves of the great golden gates of his courtesy had swung them slowly open. There was nothing for me to do now but enter.

"Madame la duchesse de Saint-Simon will be only too delighted to serve you, sire!"

The king at once signaled his attendants to turn his wheelchair back to his entourage, and he made the announcement then and there, both of the marriage and of my wife's appointment. I did not even have the chance to speak to Gabrielle before she became the mistress of a household of five hundred persons, with a larger apartment at Versailles and a salary greater than my whole income! She had proved herself the more skillful courtier, but at what kind of court? The court of absolutism and bastardy, the court that I had dedicated my life to purifying!

The king's chair was now turned back towards the palace, and behind it, people crowded up to congratulate me. Some, I suspected, were sarcastic, but the majority meant well enough. We had all, I could only conclude grimly, been made parts of the Versailles system.

7

I T WAS not long after these events that the royal family was struck with a series of deaths that seemed to threaten its very survival. First Monseigneur died, at the age of fifty, stricken with smallpox, and the entire court gathered at midnight at Versailles to watch the return of our ancient monarch from his son's deathbed at Meudon. As the reader can imagine, this news was hardly dire to me. At a single stroke, all the elaborate plottings of Madame la Duchesse and her cabal were swept away. The only thing that astonished me was the attitude of the duc d'Orléans, who wept genuine tears of regret for this cousin who had so hated and persecuted him. I urged him to take his sorrow to the privacy of his chamber, for he was bound to be accused of the most odious hypocrisy.

But the next blow was far, far worse, the greatest tragedy that France has had to sustain in my lifetime. The charming, the enchanting duchesse de Bourgogne suddenly sickened and slipped away from us, followed in a few days' time, horror of horrors, by her inconsolable husband and the elder of his two infant sons, the duc de Bretagne. The king had lost three heirs apparent in less than two years, and the succession now depended on the fragile life of an infant. Who would be regent? Presumably the stupid Berry! And then *he* died, childless, as a result of a riding accident, leaving the king (except for the Spains) with a single delicate two-year-old boy for all his legitimate posterity! Even I began to have sinful doubts about a God who allowed the bastards so to multiply and the licit issue to wither on the vine.

A silver lining to our cloud of woe was the still tighter unification of all classes of our country around our stricken and embattled old sovereign. The allies had missed their opportunity, and when the Treaty of Ryswick was finally signed to end the most devastating of all wars, we found ourselves, however exhausted and impoverished, still in possession of the bulk of the territorial advantages gained in the king's earlier campaigns. And, of course, Philippe V remained king of Spain, although this, as I had long suspected, turned out to be no great advantage to our country.

I had hoped to find another silver lining in the rise of the fortunes of the duc d'Orléans, who had every claim now, as second heir to the throne, to act as regent for the infant Louis XV, Bourgogne's second son, when the latter should succeed. Yet this prospect was muddied by the absurd but persistent rumor that Orléans had caused the duc and duchesse de Bourgogne to be poisoned. Anyone who knew him knew how incapable he would have been of poisoning the devil himself, but people *didn't* know him, or understand him, and his laboratories at St.-Cloud and the Palais-royal were regarded by the superstitious as embassies of hell. I have no doubt that Madame la Duchesse was heaping brushwood on the fires of suspicion; it was rumored that the king himself, convinced by the ever-vindictive Maintenon, had not rejected the accusation out of hand. I cannot emphasize more strongly how bad the situation had become than by pointing out that, in the most sycophantic of courts, the king's own nephew and second heir to the throne, the probable future regent of the land, was shunned by all but the Saint-Simons!

In the meanwhile the bastards were at work again. It began to look as if their hour might strike at last. Madame la Duchesse and Madame de Maintenon became passionate allies in promoting the regency of the duc du Maine. Madame de Maintenon, Gabrielle reported to me, usually so tactful with the king, was now positively shrill in her arguments that only this pretty bastard son, the king's favorite of all the litter, could save the House of Bourbon from extinction and oblivion. I felt that my old nightmare was at last coming true.

The news broke like thunder one hot summer morning that the king, by simple edict to be registered with the parlement of Paris, had raised the duc du Maine and the comte de Toulouse to the rank of princes of the blood with rights to succeed to the throne on the extinction of the older branches! When I rushed to our apartment to tell Gabrielle, I found that she already knew. But she seemed, as usual, perfectly composed.

"What you must do immediately is call upon the duc du Maine and congratulate him. Everyone is going there. Let's not be the last!"

I stared. "Do you really expect *me*, Gabrielle, having held all my life to the principles of which you are well aware, to be guilty at this point of such an apostasy?"

"It's not an apostasy, Louis; it's a form." Gabrielle had taken to using my Christian name ever since she had become a lady of honor. "If, in the new reign, Maine should be the ruling force, this will have been your chance to make up for all the snubs he's suffered from you. If not, it will be only a bit of politeness that nobody will remember."

"Except *me*. It would be a dead weight on my conscience!"

"Really, Louis, you're being even more unreasonable than usual. You owe it to Maine as a family matter. After all, he's your cousin."

"I do not acknowledge him!" I cried indignantly. Never before had Gabrielle dared to fling in my teeth that Madame de Montespan had been a cousin of my mother's, relating me, indubitably, to her illegal as well as her legal spawn.

"You can't just think of yourself in these matters," Gabrielle continued inexorably. "You must think of your sons. Why should you deny them their place in the sun? It's all very well for you to say that you'd rather die than live in a France where Maine was king . . ."

"King!" I almost shrieked. "Do you have to go that far? We're only talking about a possible regency."

"Not at all. We've had four deaths in the direct royal line since 1711. How many more would we need, under the new edict, before Maine succeeded?"

I did not have to count, but I did, to prolong the agony of having to answer her. The weak baby dauphin. Orléans and his little boy. The young duc de Bourbon and his two younger brothers. The young Conti. "Seven," I almost whispered.

"And most of them mere boys who haven't had the pox. Oh, it could happen, Louis. Besides, how do you know that the king, now he has the bit in his teeth, won't put Maine *ahead* of the young Condés and Contis, distantly related as they are and hardly known to the public? Maine is his son — the son of Louis the Great!"

I decided that there was no point arguing further the rights or wrongs of the matter with Gabrielle. There were issues that the female of our species simply could not — or would not — see. Had Gabrielle found herself transported in time and space to the court of Attila the Hun, she would have found no difficulty in qualifying as lady-in-waiting to one of his concubines. But her words about our poor two undersized boys, the "beagles," as they were cruelly known at court, cut deeply into my heart. Should I sacrifice them to my principles? Was I being selfish in my idealism? I had stood by while Gabrielle became lady of honor to Madame de Berry. I had even fostered the Berry marriage. How could I make my sons pay *now* for such scraps of ideals as I had left? I should have been hanged for a lamb!

When I presented myself at the apartment of the duc du Maine, I found it jammed with a noisy, congratulating crowd of courtiers. Yet such was my reputation for being anti-bastard, that something like a hush fell over the room as the pretty little duke hurried towards me with outstretched arms.

"Saint-Simon, my dear fellow, I'm so delighted!"

Even I had to concede that his eyes recalled the beautiful ones of his late (O God!) half-nephew Bourgogne. No one was less sincere, no one more demonstratively affectionate, than this love child of the Montespan. I choked so that I could hardly speak.

"I have come to offer my congratulations on your elevation, sir. May you live long and prosperously to enjoy it!"

The bastard now actually embraced me. "It means all the more to me, Saint-Simon, in that the duchess and I believed you antagonistic to the edict."

"Allow me to explain that, sir." I was well aware of the openly smirking members of my acquaintance who moved closer to hear how I should get out of *this* one. Well, I would show them! "I have been opposed only to the intermediate rank created for you and your brother between the princes of the blood and the peers. I had thought there was neither precedent nor justification for it. But now that the king has seen fit to correct this by increasing the class of princes of the blood, I can think of no more appropriate addition than yourself."

At this I thought it best to retire. The ingenuity of my excuse aroused considerable hilarity at court, but I had long since learned how quickly these things passed. I prided myself on having got out of a bad situation as best I could.

Gabrielle, in the meanwhile, had her hands full with the duchesse de Berry, who, since the death of the duchesse de Bourgogne, had become first lady of the land. I wonder if, since Messalina, any great princess of an imperial court has behaved so grossly. She not only drank to excess and used the foulest language; she made hardly any secret of her lovers, some of the lowest class. As even she would hardly have dared to behave so at Versailles under the eye of the king and of Madame de Maintenon, she spent most of her time at the Luxembourg, which had been given her as an official residence at Berry's death. Gabrielle ran this great establishment and ran it with the greatest efficiency; it was thanks to her that the public scandal of the duchess's life was not worse than it was. She occupied a beautiful apartment on the main floor of the palace, where I would sometimes join her for a week at a time.

"At the pace the duchess is going, she won't last long," she told me. "But I shall have put aside enough to last us a lifetime."

"Isn't there anything you can do to stop her?"

"Do you think me a monster? I would if I could. No, I assure you, it's hopeless. That poor girl has the drive of Louis XIV and the passion of Madame de Montespan, all without a single compensating principle, either in religion or humanity."

Savonne and I were no longer on speaking terms. He haunted the Luxembourg, completely infatuated, drinking more and more, degraded to the point of sharing his adored princess with lackeys. Nonetheless, I was taken by surprise when Gabrielle announced to me that a *lettre de cachet* had placed him in the Bastille.

"But why?" I demanded. "Why just *him?*"

"I haven't the least idea. All I know is that it's where he belongs."

I decided that I could not abandon a lifetime friend without a further inquiry, and at Versailles I requested an interview with Madame de Maintenon, stating my concern for my friend and her cousin. The great lady gave me a few minutes before her departure for St.-Cyr. She was very old now, pale and a bit haggard, but she held herself as straight as ever, in the high red chair.

"Your wife knows all about the matter, Monsieur de Saint-Simon," she said in a cold, clear tone. "But I have no objection to explaining it to you, if she does not care to do so. The duc de Savonne has got it into his silly head that he will marry the duchesse de Berry. This, of course, is not only not to be allowed; it is not even to be thought of. The king has given orders that Savonne, *if* and when he is released from the Bastille, shall be exiled permanently to his estates. Would you suggest that the king had an alternative, sir?"

"No, ma'am," I admitted sadly. "I am only sorry for our friend."

"I am sorry for *all* of us, Monsieur de Saint-Simon. There is no point pretending that you and I are not aware of all the horrors that go on at the Luxembourg."

"It is indeed a tragedy. Who could have guessed that that charming child should have turned out so?"

"Your wife could have guessed it!" Madame de Maintenon exclaimed sharply. "Or rather, she knew it all along. She was aware from the beginning of the viciousness of Mademoiselle de Valois' character. But what did your wife care for poor Berry? All she cared about was to be lady of honor. Well, I suppose she's no worse than half the court. That's what we produce, here at Versailles, while we perish in symmetry!"

"Madame, I must protest! You are not fair to my wife!"

"Oh, Monsieur de Saint-Simon, go away, please. I'm an old woman, and I'm tired. You have twice interfered with the royal family, and I hope you're proud of the results." She put up her hands emphatically as I was about to speak. "That will be all, sir!"

Gabrielle was at our apartment at Versailles that day, so I did not, dizzy with grief and confusion as I was, have far to go to confront her. But she simply sighed when I blurted out the story of my interview, as if it were almost too much, with all that she had to go through, to be obliged to refute such naïvetés. When she spoke at last, it was in no tone of apology.

"Of course, it sounds cold-blooded, put that way. I *did* have a pretty good idea that Mademoiselle de Valois was a bad lot. But what was the alternative for poor Berry? Mademoiselle de Bourbon was not much better. Besides, Berry had been so badly educated, in that idiotic way they treat younger sons, that he would have been an easy dupe for any clever Bourbon princess. It would have been easier had there not been a war. Then he could have been matched with some docile German cow, and I promise you I would have been glad. But as it was, the poor fellow might as well marry where it would do *us* some good — you thought so yourself — "

"I did it for Orléans!" I cried in exasperation.

"Well, it comes to the same thing. We stand with the Orléans. And at least Berry had some wild nights. For that little bitch gave him a good time, I promise you. Oh, yes! He had *that*, after all, in his short, useless life. And it's about all he did have. No, Louis, I apologize to no one!"

"Gabrielle! I want you to resign your post! I can't have you working any longer for that creature!"

I had risen in my anger, and she rose now, too, but she was as calm as I was excited.

"I shall resign my post when the king asks me to, and not a minute before. So direct your plea to him, if you dare. And let me say this. I have given you every chance through the years to make a position for our children, and all you have done is dissipate our assets. You have achieved neither post nor honor. You have spent your life jumping up and down in idle protest against a great king. So I had at last to decide to do things my own way. I managed to secure the money and position the children need. I hedged my bets against the future. Whatever happens in the new reign, we shall have our chance. Leave me alone, Louis. Leave me to do things my way. I always promised that I would help you. I still think I have!"

"And what do you leave *me?*" I cried in misery.

"I leave you the last word. *Write* about us. We shall have existed only for you!"

8

A ND THEN the unthinkable thing — or rather, the only thing
about which we had been thinking — happened. The king
died. On September first, 1715, after the longest reign in recorded
history, seventy-two years, Louis XIV bequeathed the throne that,
even after the terrible reverses of the Spanish war, he had made the
first of the civilized world, to a child of five. I, with hundreds of
others, silent and awed, had watched him, day and night, to the
very end, stiff, formidable, unable to eat and hardly to drink, re-
fusing until the last minute to abandon his rigid routine. He had
lived on stage, and he died on stage, never out of character, never
missing a cue.

Why do we ever worry about the future? It may be better than
we have hoped, or far worse than we have dreaded, but we can be
sure that it will never be what we anticipated. That was the lesson
I learned in the first years of the new reign. I had been quite ac-
curate in surmising that Madame de Maintenon and the duc du
Maine would have prevailed with the dying old king to leave a
will conferring the governorship of the young Louis XV and a
seat on the regency council upon Maine, but what I had *not* predicted was that the duc d'Orléans should have persuaded the
parlement, without the slightest difficulty, to invalidate the testa-
ment and recognize his absolute regency.

Even better things were to come. The regent, who had kept his
old antagonism against the bastards more alive than I should have

thought likely in one so easygoing, now proceeded to direct a supine parlement to strip the duc du Maine and the comte de Toulouse of their status as princes of the blood, to deny them and their issue all rights of succession to the crown and to reduce them to the peerage, ranking them only with the dates of their titles. At last I took precedence over the wretched Maine, and the day of his humiliation, when I caught his shame-faced eye with my own triumphant one across the chamber of parlement, was perhaps the most glorious of my lifetime.

Gabrielle was never a woman to indulge the mood of "I told you so." All she said, when I returned from the ceremony, was "So there's your dragon — all paint and smoke." And after that, very wisely and kindly, she did not refer to the matter again.

We were tranquil together once more, she and I, in those early days of the regency. Our differences had disappeared. Orléans, who was as hopeless a parent as he was capable a statesman, allowed his favorite child to do anything she wanted, so Gabrielle no longer had to make efforts to keep her respectable, and was able to confine her task as lady of honor to the remunerative business of running the Luxembourg. Versailles had been closed, and the young king moved to the château de Vincennes, so the capital of France was again Paris, or rather the Palais-royal, to which I repaired almost daily as a member, appointed by Orléans, of the great regency council. I had re-occupied my comfortable hôtel in Paris, for my mother, now very old, preferred to live in La Ferté. It was, on the whole, a good life.

So why should I have not been indefinitely contented? We had weathered the crisis of the great king's passing. The bastards had been put in their place. Orléans had been restored to his rightful position. The young king had improved in health and was beautiful to look upon. Why was not all for the best in our fair land of France?

The answer, I think, lay in the complicated character of Orléans himself. He was wise, shrewd, quick-witted and generous. He was totally devoid of vindictiveness. He allowed Maine, once reduced to his proper status, to keep all his wealth and other honors. Even those who had wickedly conspired against the regent were let off with simple admonitions. Hardly a day went by at the Palais-royal when I did not see him sign a pardon or mitigate some ghastly punishment. In foreign affairs he adopted the healthy policy of healing the open wound between England and ourselves, and he made every effort to conciliate the suspicious and still resentful king of Spain.

Yet he was like the child in the fairy story who had received every gift but the knack of coordinating them. What seemed to me his deepest deficiency was in any real faith in himself, or in the House of France, or in God. It was as if he were playing a part, and laughing at us for trying to believe in him. I suspected that the only times he considered that he was actually living were when he retired in the evening with a group of debauched friends, including, alas, his Messalina of an oldest daughter, behind doors that were not to be opened except in the direst emergency, and dined and wined and God knows what else, waited on by handsome servants of both sexes, until the small hours. How could these orgies not have affected the morale of our government from top to bottom?

Of course, they did. The word "regency" to this day has a ring of free living, loose manners, godlessness. And then, too, the regent's stubborn passion for experimentation was productive of disaster. It was he who encouraged that wily Scot, John Law (whose surname should have been just the opposite), to launch his Mississippi Company, which embarked the whole nation on a torrent of inflationary spending. Nothing could have been more destructive of the ordered hierarchy of our society. I had always supposed that if our system were ever to be toppled, it would be by a revolution, as in England, when the Puritans had cut off the head of Charles I, great-great-grandfather of our own infant king. But now I saw that violence and bloodshed would not necessarily be required. With inflation a lackey could become a millionaire, and a duke a bankrupt. The figures did it all.

But when I protested to Orléans about what the world was becoming, he would simply laugh at me.

"Really, my friend, do you think I can change the shape of history? You are very flattering. Even my uncle could not do that."

When arrangements were made to marry his daughter Mademoiselle de Montpensier to the prince of the Asturias, heir to Philippe V, I asked Orléans if he would appoint me to the post of special ambassador to escort the young princess to Madrid.

"I can't imagine a better man for the job!" he exclaimed cheerfully. "You're the only person who can beat the Spaniards in etiquette!"

Gabrielle had no idea of making the arduous trip to Spain, and she objected to the immense personal expenses to which I would be subjected. When I pointed out, however, that my real objective was to obtain the rank of Spanish grandee, which under the circumstances Philippe V could hardly refuse me, and confer it on our second son, she withdrew her objections.

I have described my journey with the moody, truculent little princess in my memoirs, so I need not repeat it here. But what I wish to emphasize was the effect upon me of the ceremonial of the court of Spain. At first, it seemed as if I had died and gone to heaven. At the Escorial, at the royal palace in Madrid, at Aranjuez, amidst a splendor as great as any at Versailles in the old days, huge numbers of perfectly attired gentlemen and ladies attended their sovereign with the ease and smartness of well-drilled troops. Everyone seemed to know his exact place and his precise duty, and disputes, if any, were legally, if a bit lengthily, processed. An air of exquisite courtesy pervaded the court, so much so that I wondered at first why these Latins had such a reputation for passion, hot blood and duels. In time I learned that all these latter things indeed existed, but that they had been woven into their proper places in the great tapestry of etiquette.

When the preliminary ceremonials were over, and the slow work on the marriage papers commenced, I began at last to learn the heavy price that the Spaniards had paid for the perfection of their forms, and I even found myself yearning for what had seemed to me the slapdash methods of the Palais-royal. And by the time we had signed terms that had really been agreed upon by correspondence long before my departure from Paris, I was in a mood (though I had obtained my grandeeship) to see the Iberian court as a mere caricature of my ideal. This in turn raised sad doubts about my own lifetime involvement with rules and precedents. Oh, yes, under that hot Spanish sky I had misgivings as well as headaches! It was not a happy time.

And then came the curious episode, the aftermath of which constituted, in some curious way, my redemption. When I went to take my leave of Mademoiselle de Montpensier, the future queen of Spain (poor child, she was to be it for a short enough time), I found her standing on a dais, surrounded by her new ladies. As I approached and bowed low to ask her if she had any messages for her parents or for her grandmother, she simply stared at me for a moment and then opened her mouth and gave vent to a resounding belch!

It was followed by another and then another. In the burst of rude laughter that now riotously filled that sedate chamber there was nothing I could do but simply turn and take to my heels. It was as if those belches and those shouts of laughter had been sweeping me out of court and out of Spain, sweeping away the whole meretricious fabric of our civilization. Could I survive this vivid protest of a lonely child, exiled forever from her friends and family, married off to a stranger, to be buried alive in a frozen court where so many French princesses before her had eaten out their hearts in sorrow and died young, to be encased in massive marble in the subterranean vaults of the Escorial?

Fortunately, I had a long voyage home and the chance to make many reflections. The most important of these was that if the present, or the future, which so mocked me, was represented by a belch, it could not be anything that I had to regard as much superior to my own lares and penates. That one way of life may have been shown up as inadequate did not mean that the first substitute at hand was any better. Was the belching little princess of the Asturias, or her drunken promiscuous older sister, any better, for that matter, than her splendid, adulterous grandmother, Madame de Montespan? Even if I should have to concede that, moral for moral, the regency was no worse than the great days of Louis XIV, at least the sinners of that older time had had style. And wasn't style a hedge against chaos? Mightn't it be, at the very worst, our only one?

When the terrible czar Peter had visited Paris after the death of the old king, he had insisted on seeing Madame de Maintenon. He was told that she lived in absolute retirement at St.-Cyr and received no one. Nothing daunted, the giant Slav pushed his way into the convent school, stamped into the great lady's chamber and yanked aside the curtains of her bed. For a long, grim silent moment the barbarian of the north and the octogenarian dowager stared at each other. Then he let the curtains drop. Two centuries had come face to face. It was a question as to which had had the upper hand.

Thinking of this episode in my bumping carriage on the rough white roads of northern Spain, I felt a new compassion for the memory of old Maintenon. The past jogged along with me as I tried to doze, popped in at me through the windows: Conti, Monsieur, the duc de Beauvillier, Madame la Duchesse, my old father, the king. Yes, it was the king who filled my imagination at the last. It seemed to me as if I might have been nothing, all my life, but the reflection of him. His terrible faults were always present: the overbuilding, the overfighting, the bigotry, the hideous persecutions, the elevation of the bastards — certainly, these things never should be and never would be forgotten. But now I began to have my vision of what the old man had nonetheless accomplished for France and for history. He had had a great style.

By the time we had crossed the border back into France, my spirits had risen, and on the long road to Paris they approached something like elation. I saw now what I was going to do with all the multitude of my notes and diaries and tracts and essays. Yes, I would, as I had always vaguely planned, mold it into a kind of history of the France of my time. But it would now be something much more. It would be a study of absolute power, exercised over a long lifetime by one man for only one goal — glory.

What it would be in the end — an epic, a history, a novel, a saga — whether it would ever even be printed, I did not know and I almost did not care. What I now *knew* was that it was my destiny to write it. It would have a kind of reality of its own, just by existing. Perhaps the day would come when it would be truer of the age than the facts themselves. Perhaps the age of Louis XIV would be created by my own pages! But the great point was that those pages had to be written.